PURE
BRONX

MARK NAISON PhD
MELISSA CASTILLO-GARSOW

AUGUSTUS
PUBLISHING

WHERE
**HIP HOP
LITERATURE**
BEGINS

AUGUSTUS
PUBLISHING

This is a work of fiction. Names, characters, places, and incidents are products of the author's imagination or are used fictitiously and are not to be construed as real. Any resemblance to actual events, locales or organizations, or persons, living or dead is entirely coincidental.

© 2013 Augustus Publishing, Inc.
eBook ISBN: 9781935883449
Print ISBN: 9781935883418

Novel by Mark Naison PhD and Melissa Castillo-Garsow
Edited by Parijat Desai
Creative Direction, Design and Inside Photography by Jason Claiborne
Cover Photography by BigAppleModels.com

Augustus Publishing paperback November 2013
www.augustuspublishing.com

ACKNOWLEDGEMENTS

Pure Bronx is the first novel for both authors and there are three people without whose support and inspiration it never would have come about.

The first is Kristina Graaff, the brilliant street lit scholar who co-taught the graduate course at Fordham where the idea for this book originated. It was not only Kristina's unsurpassed knowledge of Urban Fiction that created the atmosphere of excitement in our class which allowed us to dream of writing this, it was her contacts with street lit authors and publishers which gave us the capacity to bring the project to fruition once we started writing.

Two of the people whom she invited to speak to the class, Jihad Uhuru and Anthony Whyte, were each indispensable to the writing and publishing of Pure Bronx. Jihad was not only the first person of stature to tell us we had a publishable manuscript, he edited some of the chapters, helped us add essential characters, and found us an editor to get the manuscript in publishable form. He could almost be listed as a third author of the book. Anthony Whyte came into the picture when another publisher broke a contract with us, not only agreeing to read the manuscript, but becoming a powerful champion for the book as well as its publisher. Anthony and his partner, Jason Claiborne, have worked with us patiently on each phase of the publication, from editing, to promotion, to cover design to make sure that when it finally appears, it is going to be a new departure in the world of Urban Fiction and a symbol of its coming of age in the academic community.

Finally, we want to thank all the students in our 'Hip Hop Street Lit Narratives" class at Fordham who supported this project from the outset and have cheered us on along the way, especially Unique Ebony Mills, Noel Wolfe, Kathleen Adams and Gina Amezquita. Your enthusiasm helped keep us going during the times it seemed this book would never see the light of day.

On a personal note, Melissa would like to thank Mark Naison for taking her repeated "Hell no's" as a yes and pushing her meet deadlines, go for a PhD, and write this book! I am so grateful for your encouragement and unwavering belief in my abilities.

"I don't give a fuck 'bout your faulty mis-happens,

Nigga we from the Bronx, New York ... shit happens,

Kids clappin'; love to spark the place,

Half the niggas on the block got a scar on they face,

It's a cold world, and this is ice,

Half a mil' for the charm, nigga this is life."

Lean Back

Fat Joe

CHAPTER **1**

Khalil walked slowly toward the playground, gripping the handle of his .38, his handsome face barely visible under his black hood. Just over six feet tall, dark-skinned and powerfully built, Khalil was a striking figure in the close-knit world of the Patterson House projects. The four-inch scar under his right cheekbone made women smile and men tremble. Even though he was barely twenty, his arrival anywhere brought people to attention.

Shivering from the cold, Khalil felt his anger mount as he walked past the rusted, rotting benches in the PS 18 schoolyard toward the ugly little playground where his best customers normally gathered. Two men stood over a ragged group of men and women seated near a sandbox that most families avoided. Damn, somebody's fucking with me, Khalil thought, knowing they had to be dealers, since cops, like everyone else near Patterson, conceded the PS 18 playground to crack-heads and junkies on weekdays and in winter.

"Dumb niggas about to learn a lesson," Khalil muttered under his breath. "They 'bout to discover that only Patterson niggas can work Patterson territory," he shook his head.

Khalil entered the west entrance of the playground just to get a better look at the men. They were short, standing about five feet six inches. The sounds of their voices reached him, and he heard a Spanish different from the kind spoken by the Puerto Ricans he had grown up with in the projects.

"Mexican niggas," Khalil said under his breath.

Then he spat on the pavement and quietly moved through the playground. His sneakers barely made a sound on the rubberized pavement the city had put there to protect falling children. Sitting on the benches, his customers watched his approach without taking their eyes off the two animated men holding court. Suddenly the man closest to Khalil fell to the ground screaming. Blood was pouring out of his leg.

"Nigga, you done," Khalil said, taking the other Mexican out before he finished his statement. "You're finished motherfuckers."

Khalil stood over the two men with his gun now resting at his side and said, "When these motherfuckers come to, somebody let them know who runs this shit. Let them know the next time they show up in Patterson, they'll leave in body bags."

Putting away his gun, Khalil looked at the crowd of frightened addicts huddled around the sandbox.

"I hope you didn't buy anything from these fools," Khalil said, gesturing with his gun.

"No, no, no Khalil," said Rose, shaking her head back and forth.

Khalil glanced at the painfully thin, older woman. He knew she was lying, but felt a twinge of compassion for the once-beautiful fifty-year-old woman. Her scarred and battered face displayed several missing teeth. Back in the day, Rose helped his mother raise him, looking in on him while his mother worked the night shift. Then crack turned Patterson Projects into a hellhole even the police avoided.

"We know better than that. We only do business with you. Besides," Rose said, pointing to the two men, "They was on some new-sheriff-in-town bullshit, and everybody knows who runs Patterson," she continued.

Khalil walked over to a forty-five-year-old Puerto Rican man. Also toothless, he sat on an adjoining bench. In the days of Guy Fisher, he once was the most feared member of the legendary dealer's crew. That was before Fisher was sent upstate for life. Now, he was just another Patterson junkie.

"Que pasa, Santo," Khalil said. "Who are these Spanish niggas and why they crazy enough to try and sell in the Patterson?"

"They new to the Bronx, Khalil," Santo said. "They living over in those buildings on 138th and Alexander."

"The ATM?" Khalil asked. "Get the fuck outta here. That shit is little Mexico. I guess they tired of niggas goin' up in their buildings and robbing them. Now, I'm really confused. Damn—what those niggas went to Oz, and get heart from the wizard? This ain't like them at all."

" I don't know Khalil—we warned them, but they wouldn't listen," Santo said.

"Look, I know you all are hurting. I'll take care of you when I get back," Khalil said, remembering his two younger brothers were standing by the elementary school, less than one hundred yards away. "I got to take my brothers to the Patterson Center. After that, I'll slide through, and drop you off a dub of that Osama Bin Laden."

"Is it the same shit that killed Fat Jack the other day?" Santo eagerly asked.

Glancing skeptically at Santo, Khalil knew better than to admit anything that might incriminate him. He nodded and winked. The floodgates opened without Khalil asking for any further details.

"Them cats are connected. El Diablo, El Dios."

"When did the Devil Gods move in to the Bronx?" Khalil asked.

"Dunno," Santos said, shrugging his shoulders.

Khalil stood up. "That Mexican bullshit is weak. Niggas want that China White. They bring that brown bullshit up here, and shit going to get real stupid. If there weren't so many witnesses..." Khalil paused, letting the unfinished threat linger in the air.

Everyone within earshot knew exactly what he wanted to say. Although he'd never been charged, it was well known that Khalil would kill anyone he deemed to be a threat to his mini-drug empire.

"I told them that shit don't fly in the Bronx. They wouldn't listen," Santo said.

Khalil walked back over to one of the men. He was little by little trying to stand. Slowly and methodically Khalil began stomping on the injured man's ribs. He heard the bones snapped then he walked over to the benches.

"Anybody see who did this to those two chili-shittin' motherfuckers?" he said, addressing the onlookers.

None of them had moved an inch from their original position, and remained seated on the benches, staring steadfast at Khalil's calm demeanor.

"I ain't seen shit, and ain't heard shit," Rose said, pointing to the man agonizing in pain, next to his friend. "They was like that when I got here."

A concurrent wave of nods surfaced from the fiends on the playground. Khalil turned back to his two younger brothers. He had left them on the other side of the schoolyard, near the old elementary school that had served Patterson Projects for more than fifty years. Even though they looked on with awe and respect, Khalil sighed. He never wanted them to see this side of him, but what could he do? If he had given the Mexicans a pass, even for an hour, it would be a sign of weakness. He would be the one lying on the ground.

Rose took a couple steps toward Khalil and whispered, "Khalil, I done known you since you was knee-high to a grasshopper. I took care of you when yo' momma was still working. And I done watched you. It broke my heart to see the streets get you, but they don't have to be you. You play the game good, so good, that I might be the only one who know that your heart ain't stone. You got a conscience and that gon' get you killed before long. Get out the game 'fore it claims you. You listen to old Rose—you hear me now?"

Rose looked at him so deeply that it caused him to turn away from her stare. She was right, and he knew it.

"'I'm getting out. I just haven't figured out how yet," Khalil said.

He started walking toward his brothers, ten-year-old Keyshawn and Kenyatta who was eight. The two boys stood shivering on the west side of the schoolyard near Morris Avenue. Khalil felt a sharp pain in his stomach, and a pounding sensation rang loudly in his head.

It wasn't that he was worried about getting arrested. The police never even entered PS 18 playground. It had been the drug marketplace for

Patterson Projects since the days of Guy Fisher, a drug lord who rose from Patterson to own the Apollo Theater. Then the Feds took him down, and threw him into a life bid.

Khalil was concerned about Kenyatta and Keyshawn. He knew that as long as they lived in Patterson, nothing could stop them from becoming drug-dealing thugs like he was. There was no innocence here. By the time a person was Kenyatta's age, you had already seen shootings and beatings. You would already know to duck when gunshots were fired. Adults in every stage of rage, nakedness and addiction wouldn't be anything new.

By middle school, where Keyshawn would be next year, one had to join a gang or crew. That was the alternative to being beaten and robbed everyday for the foreseeable future. It didn't matter how well one did in school. The hood had first dibs, and would claim you.

Two boys ran up to Khalil as he approached. They wore huge smiles on their faces, sending a chill through Khalil. Keyshawn made a smashing motion with his arm as though he were knocking someone out with a pistol.

"You took that nigga out with one shot. He still laying there. He ain't moved,"
Keyshawn shouted.

"I liked the way you stomped them." Kenyatta screamed, stomping the ground first with one foot, then the other. "I hope they dead."

"Ain't nothing to be proud of," Khalil said. "It's just business. And it ain't the best business either. Someday, I'm getting you out of here so you don't have to do this shit."

"Nah Khalil," Keyshawn said. "We wanna be just like you. You the baddest nigga in Patterson. You get mad respect from everyone you meet."

"There are other ways of getting respect than beating people down,"

Khalil said, taking the boys' hands and walking them out of the schoolyard. Khalil tapped on the side of Keyshawn's head. "You can get respect with your brain. You can be a doctor, a lawyer, a teacher, or a scientist. You're both A-students. If you keep working hard, who knows where you might end up?"

"Mom says you were an A student," Kenyatta said. "So why ain't you a doctor…?"

"I wish I was," Khalil said. "I wish I was."

They turned down Morris Avenue heading for the hot-dog stand on the corner at 143rd Street.

"I'm glad you ain't," Keyshawn chimed in. "Everybody around here afraid of you. At school, nobody messes with me because they know you my brother."

Khalil was about to reply, but the obvious pride his brothers felt in him shamed him into silence. His brothers were right. If you lived in Patterson, it was better to have a brother who was hood certified, than one who was in college. Here it was all about survival and respect, and that only came from the end of a fist or the barrel of a gun. Unless his brothers got out of Patterson, they were going to grow up to be just like him.

Khalil decided to change the subject and said, "Look at the sky. There's a big storm coming. Let's get some hot dogs before I take you two to afterschool tutoring."

"Yay," the two brothers shouted. They were back to being kids. "Can we get sodas too?" they chorused.

"Yeah, you can get sodas," Khalil said. "Just remember that what you saw is just between us."

"We know, Khalil," the two brothers said, nodding. "We know."

Khalil walked Kenyatta and Keyshawn hand-in-hand to the hot-dog stand. They got hot dogs smothered with onions and cans of grape soda. Then they walked over to a bench, sat down, enjoying their treats. Anyone from outside Patterson who was driving by would have no doubt smiled at the family scene. There was obvious love between the handsome young man and his younger brothers. Their faces lit up with the innocent joy of his attention. Showing no sign of what had happened just ten minutes earlier, they gobbled up their hotdogs.

CHAPTER **2**

After they were finished eating, Khalil walked his brothers to the Patterson Community Center. This was where the brothers spent many evenings after school, getting tutored in math and science. It was across the street from the new PS 18 on Morris Avenue. The center was the one place in Patterson where he knew his brothers would be safe. He could leave them there for a couple of hours while he went to cop heroin and milk sugar. While Khalil was away handling his business, his mind was at ease knowing that his brothers would be studying or playing ball and that his reputation gave them protection.

It had not been that way when Khalil was his brothers' age, but that now seemed like it was a century ago instead of a decade. In the mid-nineties, the crack epidemic was still at its height and bullets were flying everywhere, even in schools and community centers. Back then, there were no safe place for Khalil to go. He couldn't go to his house, his building, nor the schoolyard, and definitely not the community center. Body bags and police yellow tape were everywhere. They were just as plentiful as the stories flying around about crack dealers taking over public libraries or picking children out of strollers, and using them as shields in gun battles. That shield madness happened in Brooklyn, where even Khalil didn't go. But the Bronx was almost as bad.

There were no wise, old heads left in Patterson to show a young blood the way. They had all been taken out by the Vietnam War, killed in drug wars or sent off to jail. Khalil was just another duck-and-run survivor, trying to stay alive and out of harm's way. But by the time he reached middle-school age, his duck-and-run days were over. The crack crews of the early 90's, such as the Purple Top Gang, had given way to bigger outfits. If Khalil wanted to get any kind of respect, any kind of protection, and any kind of money, he had to join the Bloods. They were the dominant crack gang in the Patterson Projects. Even that wasn't any real safety. The Bloods were always dividing into rival crews trying to take each other out. All of them were prey for the Syndicate, a deadly Bronx gang that made a fortune robbing dealers.

The Bronx in the 90's was like the Wild West, and it was shoot-or-be-shot for a young brother like Khalil, especially one whose mother was addicted to the very poison everyone was fighting over. The wild times stirred Khalil's memory as he walked back toward 143th Street to meet with his drug-connect.

Things had calmed down a bit, but life was still hard in the Patterson. Maybe harder because the crazy dollars that crack generated in its heyday weren't around anymore. But at least you didn't have to crouch down every time you walked by your project window, or worry about dodging bullets every time you walked to the subway or went to the corner store.

If Kenyatta and Keyshawn kept doing what they were doing, they had a shot at escaping prison and early grave. Those seemed to be the two most common destinations for young boys in Patterson. They also had something Khalil didn't have growing up, a big brother who could offer them protection. It was a hard path Khalil was walking, and he often questioned whether he would be there for them over the long haul.

With these thoughts racing through his mind, and his senses still on hyper alert, Khalil turned right on 143rd street. He walked slowly toward Julio's green Range Rover, double-parked halfway down the block.

"What up, Rashaan?" Khalil said to a teenage boy from his building he passed on the way.

"Sustainin' and maintainin', dog... Still pushin' my music..."

"That's what's up," Khalil shot back, almost walking into Mr. Jones's wheelchair. "How are you, Mr. Jones?" he said to the older man, parked by the curb waiting for an ambulance to take him to the hospital.

"You don't even wanna know, young-blood. Just cause I ain't got no mo' medical, I'm the last to get picked up, the last to get any kind of attention, and the first to get experimented on with new medicine and techniques. I'm seventy-three and paralyzed from the waist down, thanks to a stray bullet I caught in my back three years ago. Didn't have no insurance, couldn't afford it."

"Gotta run, Mr. Jones, but here," Khalil said, handing the man a twenty-dollar bill. "Catch a cab."

Khalil made sure he was polite to everyone. He knew that if you ignored people or pretended not to know them, it would come back to haunt you. This would more likely happen when it was least expected, and you were least prepared for the consequences. There was no anonymity in any project or hood in the Bronx. Everybody knew exactly what everyone else was doing. One had to stand up for what one did, be it good or bad, constructive or downright crazy.

"Hop in," Julio said, and Khalil jumped into the driver's seat next to the mature man in his early forty's.

Julio was the main heroin supplier in the south Bronx, and was rumored to own several bodegas along with restaurants in San Juan and New York. Unlike the Bloods who ran the crack trade in Patterson, Julio was a seasoned businessman and ran his operation under the radar. Violence was his last resort. The copper-skinned, silver-haired, Puerto Rican man bumped fists with Khalil.

"I've got bad news, my brother. With the Obama people sending all those troops to Afghanistan, our supply has been severely interrupted. I've only got enough here to keep your customers going for two days, three at the most. When more comes in, I'll get them to you. But I'm warning you, the price will go up," Julio said.

"Damn, Julio, we already in a recession. Hell, I can't cut that shit any more than I have, cause them Mexican niggas sellin' that mud. And to compete with they cheap prices, I got to still have the best shit on the block. This is fucked up!"

"So it is *mijo*. No matter who's president, it's hard for a brother to make an honest living. But don't worry. Things will get better. Obama will tire of Afghanistan just like the British and the Russians before him. And our supplies will come back, along with our profits."

"Julio, with all you know, you should've been a college professor, not a hustler. How the fuck did you end up like this?"

"*Coño*. Whitey don't want the Spanish man in competition with him any more he want the Black man. He knows we're tougher than he is, so he locks our ass out. And while he does his hustles for billions, we kill each other for Franklins and Jacksons. Until we wake up, that shit isn't going to change."

"You sound like the old heads in Coxsackie, Julio."

"I was one of those old heads in Coxsackie before I got out and went back to the streets. Wasn't that how you met me?"

Khalil thought of his three years in that hellhole upstate. His bid started with him being a ready-to-die Patterson soldier who was caught between the Bloods, the Five Percenters, the Latin Kings and the Aryan Nation. There were many knife fights, beefs, and a train of niggas left bleeding in showers or on cellblock floors, followed by months in solitary. But Khalil ended his sentence as battle-tested survivor, listening to the older cons holding court in the prison library. There his mind was opened to the message of peace and knowledge of self, given to him by Jihad. Jihad was a Coxsackie old head who ran the largest drug ring in the state before he had been taken down. Sentenced to life without parole, Jihad was now writing books about his experience and pulling aside younger cons like Khalil, he thought had potential.

"True dat. Jihad, my teacher upstate in the pen, was the one who told me to look you up when I got out. He said that you could set me up in a business that wouldn't kill me."

"And haven't I done that?"

"Well, I ain't caught a bullet or a case since I met you but I'm not ballin' like Diddy, either. This H money isn't like crack money, but it's still money."

Julio sighed, lightly tapping the steering wheel to the salsa music playing from his stereo. "*Mijo* that's why I leave crack to the young-bloods. Our customers just take the drug to kill their pain. You're like a doctor doling out medicine. And one time won't bother you as long as you and your customers don't make trouble. You've got the closest thing to a free pass a drug dealer can get, so make use of it. Remember this, as long as you're alive, there's always hope for a better day. Make sure you look after those brothers of yours. I hear they're great students."

Khalil reached into the pocket of his jeans and pulled out a thick bankroll wrapped in a rubber band.

"Thanks Julio, I'm on top of them. See you in a few," Khalil said.

Leaving the money on the passenger's seat, he hopped out of the Range Rover. Khalil didn't have to ask. He knew that a quarter key of heroin, with "Pure Bronx" stamped on the package would find him before he was a block up the street. Julio never rode with drugs, and never did hand-to-hand exchanges with drugs or money.

Julio had bent the curb, and was long gone when an old, heavyset, coal-black woman dropped her small grocery bag near Khalil.

"Let me get that for you, ma'am," he said, bending down and picking the bag up.

The woman was halfway cross the street when Khalil came up with the bag of spilled apples. There was a package taped to the bottom of the bag. Khalil walked toward the community center, thinking of the long and winding path that had led him to the heroin trade and doing business with Julio.

CHAPTER **3**

Rasheeda stood in front of the full-length mirror at Monica's house, examining her five-feet-seven plus frame in high heels. With the slender waist of a model, and an ass that defined apple bottom, Rasheeda knew she was an eye-catcher, especially in her neighborhood, where men whistled at anything that appeared to have female body parts.

"Wow, *chica*, you lookin' sexy," Monica said, re-entering the room from her bathroom. "You sure you wanna waste that all on Harlem?"

"What you mean, girl?" Rasheeda said, looking back at her reflection.

She smiled thinking how good she looked in a white leather mini, black tube top and black thigh-high boots. It was just how Bronx girls rolled.

The ideal became even more glamorous, when she, Monica and Cee Cee got together. They were always trying to outdo each other.

"You know I always look good, but I don't know how you can even see me with all that bling you rockin'," Rasheeda said.

"*Que?* This old thing?" Monica said, twirling in her short, shimmery silver dress and beaded heels. "Yo, Cee Cee said she'd bring some Alizé to get the party started, so finish up and get ready," Monica continued, admiring herself.

Both women strutted back and forth in the living room. They stopped to strike different poses like they were on a fashion runway. Then the doorbell rang.

"Déjà vu," Rasheeda said under her breath.

Monica pranced over to answer the door. Rasheeda loved Monica; that girl had always been down with her ever since they met at Cheetah's, but Cee Cee was another story. Monica and Cee Cee did have history. They grew up together in the Claremont Houses, and had to look out for each other just to survive. But Rasheeda still didn't understand why Cee Cee had to be such a nosey, know-it-all cunt. She couldn't stand Cee Cee, who hadn't learned to mind her own business growing up in a place where you didn't ask questions and you didn't see anything.

Monica had come a long way. She shared a neatly furnished apartment on Tremont Ave in the Bronx with her younger sister. Monica still loved that hood rat though, who at nineteen, like so many, already had two babies with two different baby-daddies. Rasheeda hadn't even wanted to go out that night, but Tuesday was the only day they all had off from work or school. Then Monica had twisted her arm, reminding her that it had been months since they had one of their girls' nights out.

Hands on her hourglass hips, and her neck dancing to the beat of her words, Monica had said, "What bitch? Now you got Khalil, you don't need your girls?"

Rasheeda couldn't really argue with the truth. Now here she was photo-shoot-fresh in her friend's living room.

"Yo, yo, what's up *loca?*" Rasheeda heard Cee Cee's parrot voice. "I just got off the phone with Deshon, and I'm tellin' you, this night's gonna be off the hook."

"Hell yeah, that's what I like to hear," Monica said her jet-black, waist-length hair swaying as she pumped her body to Nicki Minaj. Monica looked white, but definitely didn't sound or dance like it. "Yo Rasheeda, you want pineapple juice with your Alizé?"

"Sounds good," she shouted, putting the final touches of make up on her ebony, Jamaican skin.

Rasheeda strutted into Monica's living room and saw Cee Cee already flopped down, legs spread open, puffing a cigarette. Rasheeda felt Cee Cee's eyes narrowing in, searching her appearance.

"Damn, girl, you looking fly tonight," she greeted.

"Thanks, Cee Cee. How you doin'…?"

Cee Cee was dressed in short shorts, and red cutoff boots. Her red tube top was such a narrow strip it covered less than a bra would. For some sense of dignity, Rasheeda guessed, she'd at least worn a jean jacket over that outfit.

Ignoring her question, Cee Cee continued. "This night's gonna be extra fly, especially now with three girls on the market."

Rasheeda took her drink from Monica. "What you mean, girl? You know I'm with Khalil."

"Dressed like that?"

"Mind yourself, girl. Look at what you wearing."

"Yeah, but I don't got a man."

"Yeah and with two kids you never will if you keep skankin' yourself out like that."

In an instant, Cee Cee set down her drink, and walked over to within an inch of Rasheeda's face.

"Who you calling a skank," she growled.

Pushing her away, Rasheeda quietly said, "No one, except bitches that be hopping beds every other night."

Before Cee Cee could say another word, Monica walked over. She placed one hand on Cee Cee's chest, and motioned with the second hand, still holding a drink then said, "*Calma calma*! Tonight's about having fun, letting loose. We both finally off from work and Cee Cee's finally got her moms to sit with the boys."

Cee Cee still didn't move, and Monica pushed her gently toward the couch then asked, "So what's the plan, chicas?"

Regaining the center of attention, Cee Cee smiled broadly and said, "It's like this. My boy Deshon just opened up this new spot Moca in south Harlem. Today's the opening party. It's gonna be tight. There's gonna be some fly-ass Harlem brothers, you know, no more of the same ol' same ol' sad specimens. If you know what I'm saying…?"

"*Claro que si, chica,*" Monica shouted, shaking the tension loose. "I'm ready to dance up on the brown brothers—you know what I like." Monica continued, smiling broadly.

Monica and Cee Cee bumped fists. Then the chattering started about Latino men versus black men. The strategy on how to work the club that night was hotly discussed. But Rasheeda was in a whole different world. She was trying to remember Harlem. It was her first home, and the one place that sent a shiver of fear down her spine.

CHAPTER **4**

Suddenly the image of her at age nine flashed before her eyes. Rasheeda was standing over the dead body of her stepfather, Joe. She hadn't thought about it in a long time, but the mere mention of Harlem, especially south Harlem, brought back that incredible moment of violence.

It was ten years ago, and she was a scrawny, lanky, little girl, clad only in a dirty, white nightgown. Her mom never took care of, or even braided Rasheeda's hair properly. It was a messy afro. There was Joe, light-skinned, and dressed only in a pair of jeans. He had been wasted down from years of heroin use, but Joe was still a beautiful man. His high cheekbones and dimples would make any woman swoon. His charms had definitely worked on Rasheeda's mom. In those days, she'd do anything to keep Joe around. Even if that meant letting him rape her own daughter. Rasheeda had to take matters in her own hands.

As she stood over Joe's body, Rasheeda wasn't thinking about the sexual molestation. She was staring curiously at the dark red color of Joe's blood. Rasheeda was amazed at how dark his blood was, and there was so much of it coming out. Even when she stepped back, it was still flowing toward her feet. Then she heard her mother screaming.

"Nooo! Joe's gone! Joe's dead!" her mother kept mumbling.

That night they packed up and moved in with her aunt who lived in the Mitchell Houses in the Bronx. Later, they got their own place in the same building. Rasheeda had never been back in Harlem. For a while, her mom was always scared. She would cry, and started drinking. They were never questioned about the incident. No one cared about the death of a poor, black heroin addict in the Frederick Douglass Projects.

Rasheeda, in the meantime, had other things to deal with in her life. She started a new school in the middle of the year, and had moved into a new building. At first, the other girls at the Mitchell Houses looked at her oddly. Then they began to throw insults at her, and started pushing her around. Just like the Crips and the Bloods, there were also girl-gang factions that fought bitterly as young as eight and nine. In this housing area, the BB's, short for bad bitches, ruled. They made fun of other kids' clothes and features, made other girls give up their money, and sometimes they even beat down girls to take their shoes or bracelets. The leader was Nikki and she used to wear all the bracelets the BB's took from other girls as a badge of her badness. It didn't take long for them to get to Rasheeda. They started calling her "dark butt."

The other gang was the Triple C's, and they were just as bad as the BBs, but their focus was different. They were all about being sexy and desirable. The girls wore as little clothing as possible and new members went through an initiation involving publicly losing their virginity. Self-professed sack chasers, they terrorized any girls they thought of as being too prudish.

The only way for new girls to survive in Mitchell was to join a group. When Rasheeda did neither, she found herself to be a target of both. At one point, she was coming home almost daily with ripped clothes and scratches. It was totally different from her experience in Harlem. The projects she lived in there weren't gang-free, but she had spent most of her free time in Harlem's Kid zone project, where she attended an after-school program. A concerned teacher recommended the program after Rasheeda kept showing up to school covered with bruises. She was only too happy to spend as much time away from home, especially from Joe.

Rasheeda wasn't a stranger to being beaten. She had known the same situation with Joe. Again Rasheeda found herself turning inward and turning off. At times, the feeling of the little fists and nails against her body almost didn't bother her. Rasheeda rationalized that it was just her body. Not her mind. As she had done so many times in her life, Rasheeda let her body go numb. She would return home in a daze, and sit by her mother, who by that time had stopped trying to get up and get a job. Day after day, mother and daughter would sit in a daze staring at their old second-hand television.

Everything changed though, the day in the eighth grade that the Triple C's, furious at her lack of response to their taunts or beatings, organized a couple of boys to rape her. They dragged her into the alley outside the school and as the two boys approached, Rasheeda snapped. Something about one of the boys reminded her of Joe. It was as if she woke up for the first time since moving to the Bronx. Screaming like a banshee, Rasheeda tore away from the girls, who were caught by surprise by a reaction from Rasheeda in over four years of tormenting. As the boys raced toward her, Rasheeda searched around the alley. Finding a bottle, she quickly grabbed it fiercely smashing it on the head of the first boy. The boy fell to the ground while the others paused in shock.

Rasheeda held what was left of the bottle at the others. There was a haunting silence as the boy laid with blood gushing from his head onto the pavement. Still holding the bottle, Rasheeda pushed through the group and walked away.

After that, Rasheeda bought herself a pocketknife, which she made sure to display whenever she saw the Triple C's. When news of her fighting back spread, the BB's were all over her to join their group. Rasheeda just flashed her knife and shook her head. She refused to speak to anyone. They eventually gave up and accepted her silence.

With no friends, Rasheeda spent most of her time studying alone. There were no after-school programs or sports leagues, so she locked herself in her room and did schoolwork to pass the time. Her mom was out dating the entire building and with all the unsafe things going on outside, Rasheeda's tiny room was the safest place. By the end of high school, she was still feared and respected. A few more fights with girl gangs had given Rasheeda a rep as a crazy loner who was ready to die fighting. Excelling at all subjects, she was also one of the best students in the school. Math was her great equalizer: she didn't need anything fancy to do it—maybe sometimes a calculator, but more often just a pen and paper. This attitude toward education led her to study at Lehman College.

"Hey girl," Rasheeda heard Monica say.

"Yo, you a'ight?" Cee Cee chimed in.

Slowly, Rasheeda felt the world come back into focus. She glanced around at Monica and Cee Cee.

"Yo, what's wrong with your girl? Is she gonna be a space cadet all night long or what? I need a wing girl, not a head case."

"Shut the fuck up, Cee Cee," Rasheeda said fiercely. "I was just thinking back on some old times in Harlem."

"Word...?" Cee Cee said. "You know people up there?"

"Used too, but I haven't been up there in a bit."

"Damn! Then let's get this little reunion poppin'. Finish up your drinks, 'cuz I'm looking way too fly for just your female eyes," Cee Cee smiled.

Rasheeda rolled her eyes and said, "I thought this was a girls' night."

"Alright, *chicas*," Monica said, collecting the glasses. "Let's not start fighting again."

"Exactly," Rasheeda replied, winking at Monica. "Just think of it this way, since I got a man, more attention for you."

"Word," Cee Cee laughed. "Why didn't you just say that from the jump?"

"My bad... Now let's get the party started! First drink on Monica!" Rasheeda said.

"*Oye!*" Monica said.

Then she and Rasheeda followed Cee Cee out the door.

CHAPTER **5**

Early Wednesday morning, Khalil glanced out the window. He saw the heavy snow coming down, and cursed silently. Much more had fallen than he had expected. He hated December weather. It was sign of empty pockets to come during the coldest winter months. In this weather the Patterson Houses almost looked peaceful. Six inches of white powder covered the cracked sidewalks and trash-covered lawns. But it was bad for business. On days like this, Khalil couldn't do his thing over by the playground. He'd have to settle for stairwells, where the smell of urine made him sick. Maybe he could operate from inside the corner store, but he'd have to give a piece of the action to José, the owner. This would cut his profit margin to the bone.

His two brothers were sleeping in the bed next to his. Khalil glanced around at the green peeling walls of his bedroom, which hadn't been painted in years, thinking of ways to get a hold of some cash while his heroin sales were slow. Maybe he could head down to the garage at the Gateway Mall.

Whether it was a blizzard, tsunami, tornado, or earthquake, Juno got it in twenty-four-seven down at the warehouse-like chop shop in Hunts Point. This was the land that time forgot, and that the police avoided. A thirty-something Honduran, he paid ten cents on a dollar using Kelley Blue Book to put a value on each vehicle brought in. Khalil did some quick calculations in his head. A 2009 745 BMW was worth at least seventy, maybe sixty, so ten percent of sixty, worst case, was six G's. That was enough to tide him over until this blizzard let up. Hell, I could take my boo to the G Bar, get her that bracelet she was eyeing at Diamonds Plus on Fordham Road, and do it up with her like Beyonce and Jay Z, penthouse suite at the New York Hilton. Rasheeda was the best thing in his life, and Khalil felt he needed to show some appreciation.

"Time to get paid," Khalil said, shaking his head.

Pulling on his jeans, Khalil staggered to the living room. His seventeen-year-old sister, Kameeka, was asleep with her two children. Kameeka had a one-year-old and a three-year-old. She used to be a lithe teenager, but now she weighed close to two hundred pounds. She along with her kids occupied a purple pullout couch and took up half the space of the living room.

The heat in the apartment was on full blast. In the Patterson Projects, residents were subjected to either no heat at all or the steam-room effect. Kameeka slept without covers. Khalil glanced in disgust at her fat thighs and butt. Her stained, torn, red nightgown had crept up around her waist. The television played on low volume. Clothes and diapers strewn all over the floor coexisted with crumb-filled dishes, baby bottles, and half-filled cups. The whole scene made him fall into a depressive state.

Inside the kitchen, the same lime-green walls greeted Khalil. He opened the fifteen-year-old refrigerator, which made an infuriating humming sound, and looked inside. Khalil grimaced when he saw a five-day old block of cheese, and several packs of Hostess Twinkies on the top shelf. Below, there was a box of Fruit Loops, bottles and bottles of Coke, along with Fanta. There was one partially eaten platter of Mac and cheese on the bottom shelf, also a huge tin of rotting potato salad, and a whole bunch of half eaten French fries from left over Happy Meals. Khalil wished there were green vegetables and wanted a piece of fruit, but there was none in sight.

No wonder Meeka look like Shamu, Khalil thought, grabbing a Twinkie and slamming the refrigerator's door. He quickly whipped his North Face ski-jacket from the hallway closet, and eased his way out of the apartment. Using the stairwell heading to the street, Khalil was immediately hit by the stomach-curdling aroma of rotted food, urine, blood, and feces. He still preferred to use the ten-flight walk-down than taking the elevator. It was usually broken and periodically used by the Bloods, the gang which almost every boy in the Patterson Houses ended up joining in their teens.

Trudging through a lobby that hadn't been cleaned for a month, Khalil frowned then carefully stepped out the door and onto the pathway to 143rd Street. There was a layer of snow six inches deep waiting for him. On a day like this, Khalil was glad he wore a good pair of Timberland boots. They were a luxury no dealer could do without. Compared to his sneakers, they were cumbersome to run in, but if he played his cards right he wouldn't have to run anyway. Khalil touched the knife he kept in one pocket, and the small pack of tools he used for stealing cars in the other.

"This is a fucked up way to live," he muttered, shaking his head against the cold.

Khalil did two bids at Spofford Juvenile Detention Center, and one stint upstate. With Mexicans and Africans flooding the hood, and willing do any job below minimum wage, even the GED he earned in prison would not get him anywhere near a job. The three strikes law, making life in prison automatic if he ever got caught again, made him pause. In order to survive, Khalil knew he had to risk it all.

CHAPTER **6**

The wind was whipping in Khalil's face, and thoughts of the minimum-wage future haunted him as he walked up 144th street. Where would he go if he squared up and quit hustling? A trainload of ideas raced through his mind, leading him nowhere fast. Khalil saw a sprinkling of postal workers and Hostos College students in the blizzard.

He normally loved walking by Hostos and checking out the fine Latin girls. They would be outside with their tight, low-cut tops, and big booties. Laughing, giggling, they would always be talking shit in Spanish. They didn't know that Khalil understood every word they were saying.

Growing up around so many Hispanics in Patterson, over time, Khalil picked up the language. On some days, Khalil walked by Hostos and dreamed he was in a classroom flirting with all the honeys, studying to be a teacher. He had dreams of preventing kids from ending up like him, in and out of juvenile, the penitentiary, and after all that, still trapping dope. A hypocrite—who ain't…? Khalil thought, At least I know I'm fucked up.

Today, things were so bad that Khalil couldn't even dream. All he could think about was the cash Juno would give him if he brought in a new car. School had once been his thing. When he was at PS 18, he always aced his reading and math tests. He loved doing art projects, and learning about other countries. At home, his mother was on crack, and food was in short supply. There was gunplay everywhere, and Nose Dick was giving five dollars a day to be a lookout. School quickly lost its appeal to Khalil. By the time he entered Clark Junior High School, the main goal in his life was to keep enough money flowing so he could eat three meals a day. He became part of the Bloods, and the young Khalil could walk to and from school head held high. He was able to stroll through the halls of Clark JHS without worrying about being robbed or given a beat-down. Khalil's life soon became an endless round of drug sales, robberies, beat-downs, and conflicts with rival gangs. The only time his life wasn't filled with conflict was when he was locked up. Crack didn't get him killed or strung out, but twice it got him locked up in Spofford, and once he was sent upstate to Coxsackie. This was all before Khalil reached his twenty-first birthday.

Very early in his life, Khalil had learned a valuable lesson. There was no safe place for him in the Bronx, not on the streets, school, not even in his own home. He realized way back that you need a crew to hold you down. Khalil was a force in his own right. He was someone everyone feared, but without the protection of Julio's heroin network, Khalil knew he was vulnerable.

He was getting ready to go across the Concourse and walk over to west 149th Street, when Khalil heard a loud voice with a hint of African accent call out.

"Dog, what you doing so close to a college…? Bloods be thinking you studying to join the Feds."

"Fuck you, Doo!" Khalil called back, recognizing the voice of his friend, Mamadou.

"I hear Africans die in weather like this. You better run back home to Mali before yo' dick freezes. But then again, you haven't used it in years, so it won't matter."

Khalil turned around, trading fist bumps and hugs with the huge man. Mamadou was almost half a foot taller than Khalil. His jet-black face showed the trace of a grin under a gray hoodie.

"Nigga, on the real side, what you doing out today? I know you can't be sellin'."

"You right about that, Doo, but I still gotta get paid. I'm heading over to Gateway Mall to see what drops… You know what I'm sayin'?"

"You need any company, K? My pockets be empty too, and nothing much will be going on in school. Plus the honeys be wearing too much clothes," Doo laughed. "You know we Africans like our women naked, or at least as close to naked as they can get in a place like this."

"Liking ain't getting, Doo. But you definitely rob better than you fuck, so we need to do some business. Let's hit Gateway. You know two is better than one when scoping out a Beemer. Security can't see shit in this snow. You know what I'm sayin'?"

Doo nodded and followed Khalil across Grand Concourse. They walked down a hill toward the highway. Doo was part of an African Islamic family of twenty-plus people. Packed into a three-bedroom apartment, they were very close, but Mamadou had somehow managed to win the respect of the hustlers on his block. In the war zone that was Morris High School, where he had met Khalil, Mamadou carved a place for himself.

The high school was located next to Forest Projects, a much-feared rival of Patterson. It was a cross between school and a detention center. Half the students were trying to learn something and the other half were profiling or laying down their hustle game. Khalil, like most Bronx kids, fell in the second category. The Mexicans and Africans were new and knew no better than try to act as if Morris was a real school. Most of them became target practice for the Blacks, Puerto Ricans and Dominicans, who took turns ripping them off or beating them down.

Not Mamadou. He not only got a free pass from every thug and wannabee in Morris, he actually got business propositions from hustlers who never cracked a book during their entire time at the schools. Khalil went to Morris High School to take a few extra courses after getting out of Cocksackie prison. He wanted to enroll in the community college if his hustles ever left him enough time, and was intrigued by this African hustler who was so scary the Bloods, Crips and DDP left him alone. It was even more intriguing that when he approached Mamadou, Khalil found out that the huge African was an expert at stealing cars.

Without telling any of his set, Khalil started boosting cars from time to time with Mamadou. He soon learned to rely on the African's intelligence, courage and capacity to inflict harm on those who challenged him. Mamadou was a Bronx original. He was so violent he broke all the rules Khalil grew up honoring. It had helped that Mamadou reached his full height of six-five by the time he was fourteen, but it was even more helpful that he had seen rape, murder and mutilation in his hometown. The village where Mamadou grew up was an army outpost in the Malian government's war against the nomadic peoples of the Western Sahara portion of the country.

Mamadou's non-Arab Islamic family had the misfortune of being attacked by both sides in the Civil War. Before he had left for America, at age eleven, Mamadou had seen members of his family shot, hacked to death with machetes, and subjected to gang rape. He had also killed a soldier who tried to rape his mother, and had accumulated scars from knife fights with marauding nomads who had tried to steal his family's grain supplies.

By the time Mamadou arrived in the South Bronx, the only place in New York his family could afford to live, he had seen things that made anything going on in the Bronx seemed ordinary. Street thugs who came at him soon found out that Mamadou had no fear whatsoever. A train of broken noses, crushed cheekbones, and sliced ears followed Doo wherever he went. Pretty soon, he walked through the halls of Morris, and the streets of the Bronx without the slightest hint of fear.

Mamadou hungered for escape from the smothering poverty he had endured his whole life. He had managed to get his GED, and was now an honor student in community college. Stealing paid the bills and tuition fees. Doo became an expert at burglary, specializing in the warehouses and factories that still dotted the Mott Haven neighborhood. He made periodic forays into the car-theft business. Though they came from different worlds, Khalil had seen in Doo the kind of fearlessness and driving ambition he admired. He periodically joined Doo in boosting cars when drug sales were slow.

The pair walked toward the mall in silence, Khalil looked over at Mamadou and nodded. Today was just another one of those days when illicit business called. A rosier future would have to wait for tomorrow.

CHAPTER **7**

"Fuck," Rasheeda mumbled, trudging through the last block covered with snow.

It was Hump-Day, and she was on her way to work. Her mother had been all over her again about hanging out late last night. She had made Rasheeda run around all morning, to pick up this and drop off that. Tuesdays were one of the few days she could take off from her school and work schedule. The best nights to make money anyway were Wednesday through Saturday, and last night had been worth it. After she had gotten over going back to Harlem, she and her girls tore it up at Moca. For once Cee Cee had been right. The place was not only fly, but also classy. Not like the usual hood spots Monica and Cee Cee had dragged her to before.

It was two-fifteen in the afternoon when Rasheeda flicked open her Sidekick. No messages.

"Motherfucker!" she said out loud, ignoring the stares.

She wasn't even close, and now she would have to pay twenty dollars to work instead of ten. Then she'd have to stay later and make up that money. Rasheeda tried to remember that stripping wasn't so bad. It was better than some of the other things you could do to survive, but sometimes shit like paying to work pissed her off.

Since she was late anyway, Rasheeda figured she might as well have a smoke. She sighed, threw down her Louis Vuitton knock-off duffel, and sat down at the bus stop. Her eyes caught a handsome, young man crossing the street and her thoughts turned to Khalil. Rasheeda's mind drifted back a little over a year ago when she first met him. She had been hanging out with one of her regulars for a minute. That wigger always spent good money with her. A gypsy cab slowed, waving it on, Rasheeda smiled at her recollection of that night. She had watched him walk coolly away from the bar, thinking how fine he was with a drink in his hand. Rasheeda's soft brown eyes followed him. Khalil's thuggish, handsome face came into view, and she knew what time it was.

Even in baggy jeans, she could see the outline of his total package, and decided she definitely wanted to take a chance. Rasheeda was well aware that brothers like him tended to be on the cocky side. They had to be cut down a notch or two before she would even consider giving in. Otherwise, she would simply be dismissed as another sack chaser.

Against the hue of stage lights, Rasheeda was dazzling in a new white bikini top and matching thong. Her sexy outfit played perfectly off smooth, ebony skin and her long, waist-length braids. With red, green and yellow beads set on her crown, Rasheeda stood out like an African goddess. Catching Khalil's eye from the stage, she beckoned him over.

He sat in a seat next to the stage watching Rasheeda wrapping her legs around the pole while pulling her sexy body to the top. Flipping upside down, she used only her ankles as an anchor to expertly slide to the floor. Her top had disappeared when she turned to Khalil, exposing perfectly round breasts. Khalil looked on with keen interest as Rasheeda winked, crawling forward. Then she smiled playfully, revealing a small gap between her front two teeth.

"Hey baby, you mind if I try something new?" she asked.

Rasheeda didn't wait for his answer. Lowering her mouth onto Khalil's lap, she created a vibrating sensation. His drink fell from his hand, and Rasheeda knew she had him. Now all he had to do was put in work for it, and he could have her.

Rasheeda was not prepared for what happened when she took him for a private dance in a back room. Khalil turned the tables on her, and did something that made her want him as much as he wanted her. That boy wasn't only fine, but had a kind heart, and possessed a magic tongue. Sitting at the bus stop reminiscing brought a mischievous smile to her face.

"Hey girl, you off to work…?"

Rasheeda was brought back to reality when she saw her home girl, Erika. She shrugged and said, "I'm tryin' to. I would take the day off, but my mom's all up on me about the rent which is due Friday. And I got a test on Thursday that I still have to study for."

"I'm sorry, girl. How's your moms?"

"Same as always, you know what I'm sayin'?"

"Yeah, I know."

Rasheeda flicked out her cigarette, thinking how her mother must have had an especially bad night. When Rasheeda woke up, their one-bedroom apartment looked like a war zone. Jack and Jim, her mother's only faithful lovers, were spilled all over the couch. The baby was crying and crawling around the floor. She cursed herself for leaving her little brother with her mother. Last night when she had left, Junior had been in the crib. Rasheeda pulled herself up and dusted the snow off her pants.

"Hey, you think you'd have time to help me study again?" Erika asked.

Rasheeda smiled. Erika had finally quit hooking. After five years, she had walked away from her boyfriend and pimp. Erika met Trey when she was thirteen. He had been controlling and pimping her ever since. It took a lot for Erika to walk away, but with Khalil's protection and Rasheeda's support, she was even going for her GED. Rasheeda was proud that Erika was trying to get out and stand on her own. It hadn't been easy for her to find a good man. Between her no-good, raping father, and her no-good, raping boyfriend, Erika had no luck.

"You know, I'll be there, girl. I just may have to bring Junior with me again."

"Cool. Thanks, girl, you always got my back. Hey and what about you Miss College Thang…?"

"Girl, I don't know. It's like a whole different language they be speaking up there at Lehman College. I thought business was just gonna be about numbers and shit. But I don't know, it's just straight wack sometimes."

"They wack then. 'Cuz I know my girl know her bizness!"

"Thanks, girlie. I'll catch you Saturday then."

Rasheeda watched Erika walk away. Saturday couldn't come soon enough. She looked up the block to Cheetah's neon lights. The two E's weren't even lit anymore. This place was so hood, Rasheeda thought as she walked. It was still better than other things us women have to do to survive. She sighed again, reminding herself of Erika's situation. "Time to get my hustle on," she whispered under her breath as she made her way back to the dressing room.

The sign and warehouse exterior may have been a sorry-looking sight, but inside was done up real fly. Catering to both the blinged-out locals, and horny crackers who made their way all the way up to the Bronx, this was the place to go for some black booty. There were no charity cases at Cheetah's. Ray, the owner, and the bouncers he employed, made sure of that. The well-stocked bar, shiny black stage, and red velvet touches, brought out all the corporate executives who wanted to get nasty but wanted anonymity.

"Hey Fantasy, *Que pasa...*?" Rasheeda smiled as she remembered how she first got her stripper moniker.

Two years ago, after being denied financial aid at Lehman College, Rasheeda started dancing at Cheetah's. She had never stripped before, so when asked what she called herself, all Rasheeda could think of was a song by Tank that started, "*I love them girls named Fantasy, I love them girls named Ecstasy...*"

"Gracias, *mami chula*," Rasheeda said, turning to her girl, Monica. "Damn, girl, you not playin' today, huh?"

She must have spent a fortune on her work outfit, Rasheeda thought. She surveyed Monica's clothes. Known as the Miss Diva Latina of Cheetah's, Monica was styling a lacy black thong with matching bra. The two-piece was so lacy it left very little to the imagination. Monica had clearly gone out of her way with her toenails painted black and displayed in five-inch clear platforms. She had braided black and red ribbons into her waist-long, black hair.

"Girl, you know *que no juego* when it comes to my *plata*."

Rasheeda always laughed at the girl's crazy-ass way of talking. She never knew what was going to come out of this *loca boricua*'s mouth. Last night in Harlem, she convinced some guys that JLo was her aunt. Monica spun, showing off the booty that made the customers go hard at first sight. It was the type of asset that left customers running to jack-off in the little boy's room.

"Whatever spic girl… I guess I'm gonna have to step it up like you know I can."

"That's right, *negra*, bring it."

The buxom buddies shared the laugh. Monica had been the only girl who had been nice to her since they had first started, and probably with good reason. The other dancers always hated. They knew that Fantasy and Miss Diva Latina, by far, made the most cheddar. While Monica tapped into sensual, salsa dancing, Rasheeda played a raw, dangerous, beautiful hood chick. She had no idea why the Wall-street types loved her dark, black beauty so much. Rasheeda was once told that it was a sort of tribal African fetish.

Maybe it was her slightly slanted eyes she inherited from her grandmother who immigrated to Jamaica as a child. She made the best ackee and bammy with gungo-peas soup. Rasheeda still missed those days when they would pick up her grandma from JFK. Grandma had died shortly after their move to the Bronx. Rasheeda only had the memories and pride grandma showed her. But she was also blessed with the heritage that was dark skin and oval-shaped eyes.

There was no time to dwell on that now. Rasheeda had to use her gifts wisely, making enough money to keep her family afloat, and pay for her school. If only her mother could manage to keep from drinking all the rent money away.

"C'mon girl," Rasheeda said, giving herself one more glance over. "It's time to break 'em hearts."

Monica chuckled and said, "Speaking of hearts, Mr. Money Bags is here asking about Fantasy again. Damn girl, what did you do to that man to get all those private rooms?"

Mr. Money Bags, here at three in the afternoon? That's odd, Rasheeda thought. He's usually in much later. But he always tips me really good, and there are all these bills to pay, thought Rasheeda, shrugging.

"I don't understand 'em, girl, but some of them just want to feel a little street danger."

Her cellphone vibrated, and Rasheeda pulled out the Sidekick. It was saw her mother calling. She hit the ignore button, but the phone went off again. Thinking the call could be about her brother Junior, Rasheeda answered.

"Were you in Harlem last night?" her mother asked.

"Why?"

"Rasheeda just answer the question."

"Yeah, I was there for a minute so what?" Rasheeda said, playing with her top.

"So what…? So what? I got a call from Mrs. Hughes that her son said he thought he saw you?"

"Yeah, but I still don't get the big deal. That was over ten years ago,"

Rasheeda said, and felt her heart start to tighten.

"Just be careful. You know I don't want anything getting stirred up. No one's ever tried to come find us up in the Bronx. But you never know."

"Okay, Mom. I gotta work okay?"

"Are we gonna have rent Friday?"

Rasheeda felt her nerves boiling with anger and she said, "That's what I'm trying to work on now, Mom. You know I got tuition to pay too. It wouldn't hurt you to go out and look for a job!"

Slamming her phone down, Rasheeda checked her makeup in the mirror. Her thoughts raced. It had never been her that hadn't paid the rent, or the electricity, or the heating. This whole idea was getting on her last damn nerve. Sooner or later, something was gonna have to change.

CHAPTER **8**

Rasheeda checked the time. It was three-fifteen: time for Fantasy to get out there and perform. She remembered when she first met Money Bags. Although she had done privates here and there, and even a Champagne Room, he was one of her first big-time, regular clients. One week he spent ten Gs on her. Those times were getting less and less frequent. Once when he was drunk on champagne and on the street act of Fantasy, Money Bags told her he'd help her get out the hood and into the business world. He promised to help her find work at a legitimate business firm. That was the reason she had gone out with him, and even fucked his balding, overweight, white body. She smirked at the thought that he had really cared about her. Now she couldn't believe how naïve she had been. Rasheeda chuckled at the idea of a rich, white dude putting his marriage and reputation on the line just to help some black girl from the hood.

His true color began showing once she got with Khalil, and refused to sleep with anyone else. He kept telling her how stupid she was. Last Saturday night he came in with some clients. They all laughed when Money Bags presented her as trying to strip her way out of the hood. As if the idea of her 'welfare-ass' making it downtown when all she could afford was a Lehman College education was crazier than a fairytale. She shivered. Recently, she couldn't even afford that.

"Like we would ever hire anyone from the Bronx…"

Money Bags was laughing, not caring that she was just a few feet away on the stripper pole. Fantasy kept smiling even though her skin was boiling. She would let them think that they were actually real smart. Rasheeda knew that they would pay all they had to Fantasy in a private session.

"Whateva…" Rasheeda hissed under her breath, shaking off the sting.

People had laughed harder and said harsher things about her business aspirations. It was getting increasingly tougher for Rasheeda to be naked in front of a man who would make fun of her like that, and not be able to fight back. She tried to make herself believe that it was just about taking his money. Besides, getting her and her younger brother out was her number-one priority. Plus his dick was tiny. She faked it every time with him.

Not Khalil. He was something else. His lips were like magic and he actually offered to go down on her. When she finally exploded, it felt like Khalil had put some crazy voodoo spell on her.

Rasheeda strolled into the dimly lit main room and watched Candy for a minute. She was up on the pole fingering her nipples, her tongue hanging out like a sick dog.

"That's one nasty-ass bitch," Rasheeda said to no one before turning to the bar.

Candy was one of the first girls to get up in her face when the customers all started coming to her for lap dances. Rasheeda held it together even when that high-yellow trick called her a spook ho, as if she was the one who slept around for money. Rasheeda had slept with Money Bags, but that was it. She never woke up to money left on the nightstand, not like Candy and her little ho crew.

Rasheeda had a nasty temper, but she had stayed out of it until Candy threatened to call immigration on Monica's family and social services on her mother. That was the line Candy had crossed to earning a beat down. Candy fought back, pulling out a braid, but Rasheeda was able to work that night. Candy couldn't work for a week after the incident. Rasheeda hated girl fights, but at least now Candy and her crew knew she wasn't playing.

"A shot of Patrón," Rasheeda said to the bartender Joe with a wink.

Then Rasheeda chilled, and scanned the room for Money Bags. She spotted him in the corner, nursing his usual Macallan 12. Downing her shot, Fantasy sauntered over.

"Hey, baby," she said, wrapping her long, black leg around his waist.

She could feel his small dick starting to stir, but also that Money Bags was wringing his hands. He appeared to be nervous and distracted. Through small blue eyes, he glanced up at Rasheeda, her smile illuminating Fantasy.

"Hey," she said again, unwrapping her leg and sitting on his lap. "What's wrong, baby? You okay?"

Money Bags took a big swig of his drink and fiddled with his Rolex. He stayed silently fidgeting while Rasheeda continued her act as Fantasy.

"C'mon, sweetie, I'll get you a private so we can go talk," she smiled.

Money Bags grabbed her hand. "Can we just go somewhere else? Like before…?"

Rasheeda, continuing her act as Fantasy, stroked his groin area. "You know that part of our relationship is over. But I can still be here for you. Come on, I'll get us the Champagne Room. How long you got?"

"I have a dinner meeting downtown at eight."

"Okay, c'mon, baby. I'll make all your worries go away."

Rasheeda smiled to herself as Fantasy led Money Bags to the Champagne Room. At a hundred and fifty dollars an hour, she could make bank, get out of this dump early, and be back home studying. She could even meet up with Khalil. There was about five hundred dollars here for the taking. Fantasy played her role while Rasheeda's mind was in a calculative mode. Looking back seductively at Money Bags, Fantasy smiled. He was staring at her full, round ass. Maybe she could get more than five. Fantasy continued smiling. She knew he couldn't get an ass like the one she offered from any white women. They just didn't have asset like that to work with, and she meant to work it into a fat-ass tip. Thoughts of her five-thousand-dollar tuition bill had Rasheeda's mind racing. Maybe with a few hundreds, she could get them to give her another extension.

Sipping seductively on her Dom, Fantasy crossed the room to where Money Bags was texting on his Blackberry like crazy. She waited for him to finish and tuck the phone back in his front pocket before starting the show. Letting her hand slowly slide down the contours of her body, Fantasy grazed over her vagina, touching her toned thigh. Sighing like she was enjoying the smoothness of her own skin Fantasy was mesmerizing to Money Bags.

"What you need, boo?" Money Bags licked his lips, his eyes following her hands. Fantasy then finished her drink and set it aside.

"This?" she said, turning to give him a straight-on view of her full round ass. Placing his hands on her backside, she slowly lowered herself to the floor. Then Fantasy extended her body forward until he could fully examine her backside. She felt his cold manicured hands explore her ass, and thoughts of Khalil spread through her mind. Rasheeda wished more than anything for those hands to be his, and not this man's. The hand moved forward to massage her clit, when Fantasy suddenly spun around.

"Not so fast," she said, chuckling and refilling his drink. "We got time," Fantasy sat on his lap. "How's work?"

Money Bags grasped around her back, awkwardly tugging and pulling at her top. His hands felt cold against her skin, warmed from dancing.

"I don't want to discuss work. Can you just get this thing off?"

"Sure baby, relax. I just want you to relax. Whatever you need…"

Money Bags had never been so impatient with her before, but he was paying. Fantasy took of her top, displaying two perfectly formed breasts. Money Bags buried his face in her thirty-four C cups, and Rasheeda went back to imagining a life with Khalil. She wouldn't have to be Fantasy anymore, showing her nipples if she didn't want to. It was a life that one day Rasheeda vowed to have.

CHAPTER **9**

A fierce wind whipped snow in their faces as they walked by an entrance to the Bruckner Expressway, and made their way toward the new mall next to old Yankee Stadium.

"The world don't give a damn about people like us," Doo said in frustration. "My pops used to get everything we needed for our restaurant right there," Doo continued, pointing at the busy shopping area occupying the site of what had been the Bronx's largest market for African merchandise. "Now you got nothing but stores for rich people and parking for the Yankees," he observed in disappointment.

"They wanna make us disappear," Khalil sarcastically smiled. "They got a G all wrong though."

"Well, my G, it's payback time. Let's pretend we belong with these rich mothafuckas and get us a vehicle."

The two men approached the passenger entrance to the parking garage, guarded by a dark-skinned man in a rent-a-cop uniform.

"A salaam Alaikum" Doo said to the guard.

He followed up by something in is native language that Khalil didn't understand, but made the guard laugh.

"What you say, nigga? I can't believe you still talking that jungle shit here in the Bronx," Khalil said.

"It's Wolof, my G, Wolof, and I told him the same thing you told me, that this weather will make an African's dick fall off."

Khalil and Doo waved to the guard then walked up two flights of stairs and through the entrance. They entered a large square area where a sparse number of cars were conveniently parked. The floor was only about one-third filled, but after walking up and down the aisles, Doo and Khalil found exactly what they wanted, a black BMW Series 7350 Li. It had a light covering of snow on the roof, but clearly in top condition. The car was parked next to a protruding concrete wall that provided the perfect cover just in case they decided to make this a carjacking instead of the straight theft they planned.

"Nigga, do you want to make this personal?" Doo asked Khalil.

"Hell yeah. These cars are a mothafucka to boost. You gotta go through all kinds of codes to start the engine."

"Then let's wait. I'll bet we can recognize the motherfucker who owns this from a mile away."

Khalil positioned himself behind the wall, while Doo walked over to the elevator that shoppers used. Both had their cellphones out and ready. After ten minutes of waiting, Khalil got the call from Doo.

"Here she comes. Bitch looks just like Beyoncé, walking like she own the damn place. This one's going to be fun."

Khalil took a look toward the elevator and saw a tall, olive-complexioned woman. She had long silky hair and with hips swaying, she hurriedly walked toward the car. Khalil could see the outline of her full breasts clearly through her coat. His dick was harder than petrified steel. Making money always made his dick hard. This good-looking woman sashaying his way had to have long paper. The mink on her back and huge rock on her finger were evidence enough. She was preoccupied with carrying two shopping bags from Bed, Bath and Beyond, and didn't realize she was being watched and followed. Doo was stealthily tracking her from behind.

Meanwhile, Khalil approached the black Ford Explorer parked next to her car. He pretended to be fumbling for his keys. The woman opened the trunk of the car to put her bags in, and Khalil crept up behind her. Quickly he put a box cutter to her throat, escorted her to the driver's side of the car, and pushed her in. Doo then came up and entered by the passenger side so the woman sat in the middle with the two men on either side.

The victim's light brown face turned pale. She opened her mouth as if she wanted to speak, but nothing came out.

"Ain't shit gon' happen to you if you do what we say," Khalil said. "We don't want no pussy. We don't want no money. We just want the ride. But you must follow our instructions or very bad things will happen. Take her pocket book, my dude."

Doo grabbed the bag. Khalil increased the pressure of the box cutter on the woman's throat. Tears streamed silently down her cheeks, her face strained with fear.

"Now put your keys in the ignition, and start the car," Khalil instructed.

"Why are you doing this?" the woman asked. "I'm a sister just like you."

"Bitch, you ain't my sister," Khalil spat angrily. "That Black shit don't play no more. Me and mines are living two feet from hell in the PJ's, and you walking through here like you own the world. The only color I recognize is green, which you got and I want." Turning to Doo, Khalil said, "Yo, what you find in that purse?"

"Yeah, this bitch live at 223 West 138th Street. Her daughters go to some place called the Dalton School and her husband works at J.P. Morgan. These Cosby niggas livin' large!"

"Word. Well, call in all that information to our associate while I tell Miss Thing here what she need to do."

Sitting in the Explorer next to the frightened woman, Khalil could feel his heartbeat slow down. The thought of his family made him care less for the snobby high-class types. He would show her what it really meant to be a street-smart nigga. Khalil looked the woman in the eye and spoke in a menacing voice.

"You may think we just some street niggas, but we as smart as you. If you do what we say, no one is going to get hurt. If you do anything different, or if the police find us, our friends are coming after you, your husband and your daughters. We know where you live, we know where your daughters go to school, and we know where your husband works. All that info now is in the hands of our friends, and they dangerous. You hear what I'm sayin'?"

"Yes," the woman spoke shakily.

"You sure…?"

"Yes," she repeated, her water-filled eyes finally meeting Khalil's.

"Here's how it's going to go. We're going to let you out of the car, and give you your bags. While we drive the car away, you're going to walk to the elevator. You're going to wait ten minutes and walk from the elevator to the place where the car was parked. When you get to the empty space, you're going to scream 'Oh my God, my car is missing.' Then you're going to go to the nearest security guard to tell him your car was stolen, and you're also going to call 9-1-1 and say the same thing. When the police come you're going to tell them that you came here and found your car missing. That's all. Then you'll fill out your insurance forms and get your money. And you'll never see us again. You got it?"

"Yes!"

"Let me tell you who you are dealing with," Khalil said matter-of-factly. "Some niggas be looking at you, with them long legs and big titties, and forget about the car. They just want to fuck you. We all about our business… The car is what we interested in. So if you do what we say, you gonna be leaving here the way you came. You with us…?"

The woman nodded slowly and said, "Yes, I understand."

"Good. Then get out of the car, sister. And we be on our way," Khalil said, withdrawing the box cutter from the woman's throat.

He eased her out of the driver's side and walked her to the trunk. Then Khalil removed her bags, and looked into her eyes. He saw nothing but fear.

"Just walk over to the elevator. Wait ten minutes, and then make those calls. And remember, there's plenty niggas out there with nothing who want what you have."

Khalil watched the woman walk toward the elevator. He nodded then made his way to the driver's seat.

"Damn, nigger, listen to this engine," Khalil said, cranking the engine. "That's the sound of money. You got the garage ticket out her purse?"

Doo held up the stub, smiled and said, "Here it is. Now how we gonna pay for this shit? I got ten dollars, and I hope you got something, because you know it's gon' cost more than ten."

"Fuck, I only got seven. Time to hope Jesus or Allah is on our side cause otherwise we gots to crash the gate."

Khalil drove the car toward the exit sign and eased onto the narrow driveway that wound the two flights down toward the tollbooth that blocked the path to the street. Khalil put the ticket in the slot, said a silent prayer, and watched as the screen lit up with the amount $16.50. He gave the attractive Latina woman in the booth his brightest smile then passed her $17 dollars.

"Sister, how you look so good on a day this cold?"

"Ooh papi, aren't you sweet. You wanna receipt?" The woman said, blushing while giving Khalil his change.

"No mami, I don't want to clutter up this car with any useless paper. You have a nice day."

"You too, sweetie," she smiled seductively.

"Damn, nigga. What's it with you and woman?" Doo said as Khalil drove through the raised gate onto the snow-covered street. "All you got to do is start talking and they just about take off their clothes for you."

"It's the magic tongue, Doo." Khalil laughed. "The minute I open my mouth, women know that I'm a master of oral sex. You African niggas need to learn how to do that shit! Women here expect a little pleasure when they give it up!"

"Shit, you know Africans don't go down there. Damn, back home, they cut women up so they don't feel nothing," Doo said as Khalil eased the car onto the street.

"Last time I looked, nigga, this ain't back home, and you need to get with the program. Sistas want a man headed straight for the gold and not come up for air until they start screaming and shouting. That's what Eddie Murphy meant by *Coming to America.*"

"Fuck you, Khalil. No woman is going to make me go down on my knees and put my mouth on her."

"Well, my nigga, then you're going to be doing a whole lot of standing and a whole lot of waiting. Now let's get paid!"

CHAPTER **10**

Khalil drove the car slowly down Bruckner Boulevard. His head was on a swivel, eyes in search of the flashing red lights of police cars. The car looked like wealth, and Khalil thought that Five-O would know it if they ever got stopped. Luckily, the streets were almost deserted. Khalil turned toward Hunts Point where Juno's garage was located. With the thugs staying holed up in their apartments or shivering in hallways and stairwells, Khalil guessed cops decided to keep patrols to a minimum. There were some big trucks out braving the snow, but almost no cars, and no sign of police.

Khalil turned right on Longwood Avenue and took a left on Garrison. This was unfamiliar territory to him, a neighborhood where almost everyone was Puerto Rican. Definitely not a good place for a brother to walk unless you knew someone who lived there, but since Khalil was driving, he was totally relaxed. He figured if he and Doo had gotten this far without the police on their tail, they would most likely make it to Juno's garage without getting caught.

He made a right turn on Hunt's Point Ave and drove down past the tenements and stores. He cruised into a neighborhood filled with garages, warehouses, and auto-body shops. This was a place where things disappeared—cars, trucks, shipments of goods, and sometimes, even people. The police rarely ventured here. Crips, Bloods, and the Latin Kings stayed away unless they were making business transactions. The people who ran and worked these ships and warehouses were a cross section of the world's craziest killers, people from countries racked by genocide and civil war. These were people who had seen and committed unspeakable crimes. They were not the type to be messed with.

Heading toward the Bronx River, Khalil entered an area that was as deserted as any place he had ever seen. The streetlights were dim and far apart. The buildings were all two stories high, with large garage doors painted a dark color. There were no pedestrians on the street, but trucks parked every twenty or thirty feet, most of them eighteen-wheelers, sprinkled with a few tow trucks and pickups. At the very end of the block, just before he came to the street that ran along the river, Khalil spotted a two-story yellow building on his right and turned into the driveway. There a tall, thin, middle-aged man with features that looked both African and Indian, wearing a grease-stained army jacket, greeted him. This was Juno.

"What you got for me on this freezing day?" Juno asked the two young men. "Damn look at that Beamer. You don't see this model round here very often. I know you didn't find this in the Bronx. Not even drug-dealing niggas can afford a car like this."

"Blame it on the Yankees," Doo said. "We got this sucker in the Gateway Mall. Some Harlem bitch drove it up here so she could decorate her bathroom. This is what's happening over by the stadium. We don't watch ourselves, niggas like us gon' be pushed out."

"Well, if you keep bringing me cars like this, you ain't going anywhere. Drive this car to the elevator, take it upstairs and we'll settle," Juno said as he turned back toward his office.

Mamadou had met Juno three years ago when he moved from robbing warehouses to boosting cars. People in the game had told Mamadou that Juno was the only person in the Bronx who paid cash on the spot when niggas brought in luxury cars, and Mamadou learned to appreciate his reliability. Plus, as a fellow immigrant who lived inside and outside the law, Mamadou came to appreciate Juno's refusal to let anyone, be it Bronx hoodlums or the authorities, keep him from making a living.

Juno was a Garafuna from Honduras. He was from part of a community of African people who lived in the coastal region of that country. Although he was the best mechanic in the South Bronx, Juno had been unable to get a bank loan to open a garage. He was forced into the loan-sharking world to start his business. There was no way that car and truck repairs could repay the loans. So Juno became a fence. He would sell stolen parts to the very same syndicate that gave him the loan. So good was he at this business, he actually paid off the loan in five years. Juno kept on trading in stolen cars to help pay for the women he craved, and to keep money flowing to his family back in Honduras.

Khalil drove the car up a driveway leading to the second floor of the building. Juno walked up the stairs and came to the car.

"Get out," he said.

Khalil and Doo watched as he got in. Starting the engine, Juno drove fifteen feet forward then backed up fifteen feet, stopping exactly in the spot where he started.

"Come to my office," he said. "We can definitely do business."

Khalil and Doo walked down the stairs and followed Juno into a cramped office filled with pinup pictures of woman of all colors. The one thing they had in common was very large booties. There were two desks, one covered with papers, the other with tools, a small television and a wall safe. There were no guns visible, but Khalil and Mamadou knew they were there. This was the office of someone who was a skilled mechanic, a shrewd businessman, and playa to end all playas. Given all Juno was into, Khalil wondered if this motherfucker ever had time to sleep. Juno opened his safe and took out $4,000 in cash. He gave Khalil and Doo each $2,000.

"That's robbery," Khalil said. "You know that car's worth $80,000 on the market and even more for parts."

Juno looked down, tapped the .38 he always kept in his right pocket and said, "Boys, don't push your luck. You take risks for three, four hours. I take them 24/7. Four thousand dollars is more than the going rate for this car, so be happy you got this much."

Khalil wasn't going to argue. Two thousand dollars was more than he cleared selling heroin in a month, and a good month at that. Plus, he had no desire to fight with Juno on his own turf.

He fingered the money lovingly, thinking he could finally do something for Rasheeda to show her how much he cared, and to get them some time alone where they could start thinking through where their lives were going.

"Juno, you a hard man," Khalil said. "But you're all we've got. Come on, Doo, let's go. Now we paid. It's time to have a little fun."

CHAPTER **11**

It was 7:30 p.m. when Fantasy ended her act and emerged from the Champagne Room as Rasheeda. She checked her phone. Fantasy had gotten her a full G richer and Rasheeda was ready to leave. A smile spread across her face as she read the text, *G Bar/ Thurs@9:30 luv/ K.* His face and message flashed across her Sidekick. Although Khalil's messages were always short and quick, he made up for it in other areas.

Rasheeda's nipples hardened in delight at the thought of meeting up with Khalil the following night. After that first encounter in the private room when his tongue had made her feel like no man ever had, she ignored him just to make sure he was for real. She went back to playing Fantasy, giving lap dances to other patrons and working the pole. Finally, he got them a private room a second time. She knew he was serious about getting some. When they got to the room, Khalil was different. He asked her about coming up in the Mitchell Houses, her family, and her dreams. Then he pulled her close and said, "I take care of what's mines, you hear? I'm a get you outta this place, away from them crackers. You feel me?"

She didn't even feel her top slip off, but felt the delicate way in which he caressed her neck.

"Girl, you tense," he had said, while skillfully massaging her shoulders and her lower back.

It was as if he knew exactly what parts were sore from her dancing. No other man, regular customer or casual patron, had ever taken time to heal her body. Khalil paid two hundred and fifty dollars for the room that night. He massaged and kissed her from head to toe. Then he shelled out another hundred dollars more so they could leave together. Cheetah policy was that the dancers had to stay for at least five hours at a time or pay a hundred dollars to leave. Khalil didn't even flinch. He threw down a Benjamin, and told her to get her things. Then he spent the rest of the night giving her memorable orgasms.

As she made her way to the dressing room, Rasheeda took a walk down memory lane and revisited the little Times Square hotel she and Khalil spent their first night. Remembering how she worked a little of her magic, sucking his large dick while fingering her clit. Once she and Khalil finally got their hands on each other, they couldn't keep away, almost fighting to pleasure one another. It was a fight Rasheeda was happy to lose. At the time, she hadn't known where Khalil learned how to do what he did to her, but as long as he was around, she knew nothing else would do. He made her explode with ecstasy when she was with him. It didn't matter the sexual position. She had orgasms before him, after him, beneath him, and on top of him. After awhile, Rasheeda had felt like she wouldn't ever be able to walk again. It was then that she decided that fucking just wasn't fucking if it wasn't with Khalil.

The next day, she shared her experience as soon as she saw Monica. Rasheeda was beaming when she said, "Girl! I just got fucked for the first time!"

The following night Khalil called and asked her out on a real date. He spared no expense, taking her to G-Bar. They dined, drank, and talked for hours. Endless chatter was something they could always do and connect on a level that wasn't just physical. That second night they didn't even have sex. Khalil just walked her to her building and asked her what he had to do to be her man. Rasheeda remembered being speechless.

With school and work constantly in the way, sometimes it was hard to see each other, but they had become inseparable. One night walking and talking, Rasheeda finally answered Khalil's question.

"Never lie and don't cheat," she said with a reassuring smile.

She knew about his dealing, his time in prison, but she also knew why he had to do what he had to do sometimes. It was part of his life in the Bronx.

The vibration of her phone disturbed her wandering thoughts. Suddenly, she realized that she allowed Fantasy to be just standing around and biting her lip. She glanced at the cellphone and read the text from Khalil.

Yo u feel me? Tomorrow 9:30 G Bar!

Rasheeda quickly did the math. By the time she got to work from school tomorrow, and put in her five hours, it would be at least eight-thirty. Getting home, showering, and dealing with her mom, she couldn't make that time. Shaking her head, Rasheeda answered the text.

Aww boo/ tomorrow's a late one/ can we do 10? I hate to make u wait a second later K/

Even though the night was going well, Rasheeda didn't feel like working anymore. A man next to her offered to buy her a drink. Fantasy took him up on it. Already at the five-drink limit allowed by management, Rasheeda wanted another, but didn't want to pay. She hated giving this establishment any more money then she already did every time she put down ten or twenty dollars just to work. Rasheeda never used to drink so much, but recently the buzz was all that got her though acting like she was Fantasy. It helped her to be nice to the clients, especially Money Bags.

"Thanks, baby," she said. "I'm dead-tired and need me a pick-me-up," she smiled, ordering a vodka red bull.

"No problem, girl. A fine sistah like you deserves a little break too. I'm Mac."

Rasheeda looked up at the tall, slender, light-skinned man, and smiled. He was definitely older, but keeping it real in Diesel jeans and Timberlands.

"Fantasy," she replied, extending her hand.

He seductively kissed the back of her hand, and Rasheeda thought she recognized Mac from around the way. She didn't dwell on the idea. At this point, all she wanted to do was get home and find something slamming to wear. It had to be an outfit that would knock Khalil on his fine black ass. Finishing her drink, she turned to Mac.

"Thanks again, sweetie. I'll be seein' ya."

Fantasy was about to walk away when she felt the grip of a strong hand tugging on her wrist.

"Where do you think you're going?" Fantasy turned, and flashed her charming smile, but was shocked to see Mac's eyes glowing dark with anger. "Have another drink."

She tried to brush it off, sighed, and said, "Sorry, baby. I'm off now. But there's plenty of girls here, okay? I got to get home to Moms."

The strength of his weight pulled Fantasy's shapely, lithe body back down on the barstool.

"I bought you a drink, now you sit with me, you lil' money grubbin' ho."

Jumping off the chair, Rasheeda suddenly slapped the seemingly angered Mac's arm away.

"Get your hand off me. If you want a ho, go down to Willis and 137th and ask for Raul. He'll hook you up."

Rasheeda was attempting to walk away, but Mac pulled her back. He slapped her across the cheek before Lou and the other bouncers could get on him.

"Thanks, Lou." Rasheeda said, before seeing Ray. "Shit," she muttered under her breath, already feeling the swelling in her face.

Ray pulled her into the dressing room. "What the fuck was that? Mac is a good customer."

"Sorry, Ray. I was done for the night."

"What, you too good now to give a regular a little attention, what with all your rich, white customers?"

"C'mon Ray! I give laps all the time. You know that," Rasheeda said, trying to calm the situation by stroking Ray's arm. "That nigga was clearly trippin'."

Ray pushed her hand away. Narrowing his small black eyes, he said,

"Nah, you was trippin'. You off for the rest of the week."

Ray turned and quickly walked away. Rasheeda began chasing after him, pleading.

"Come 'on, Ray, you can't do that. I got bills."

Pushing her back into the dressing room, Ray said, "Maybe you should think of that the next time you turn a customer down."

Rasheeda sat down in front of one of the vanity mirrors and felt her blood boiling over in rage. Seething, her thoughts raced. It wasn't fair. Every time she thought she caught a lucky break, a good customer, an extra tip, something always tore her down. She slammed her wrists down hard on the counter, fighting back tears. Rasheeda felt the sting of things gone totally wrong. She gazed at her reflection in the mirror. Tuition bills loomed larger and her loan rejections had grown to an intolerable level. Rasheeda felt the helplessness of her situation weighing her down. She didn't know how she was ever going to get from under it. For the first time in years, Rasheeda cried.

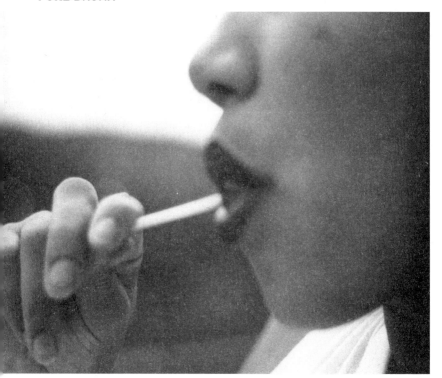

CHAPTER **12**

Rasheeda could hear the hooting and hollering from almost a block away. There were some guys lined up outside of her economics class causing the commotion. Ever since they found out she was a stripper at Cheetah's, they had been harassing her. At first she told them to shut the fuck up, but they just gathered up more guys to taunt her. They would ask for lap dances, and tried slapping her ass. She played it off by calling them "so lame" and telling them that they couldn't afford a lap dance. The harassment continued with them throwing down dollar bills whenever she came by.

"Pick 'em up," they'd order.

The girls were even worse. They simply turned a blind eye, or whispered how she deserved it for being a slut. Those bitches treated her like a freaking' prostitute, and Rasheeda knew prostitutes. They were worth a lot more than those uppity skank ho's. This was Lehman for fuck's sake, not Fifth Ave.

So that day, last March, Rasheeda had had enough. They were raining down their meager dollars and Rasheeda thought fuck it. I'll buy myself lunch at least and started picking up the money. She felt them grabbing onto her and feeling up her breasts. Rasheeda felt the sting of someone slapping her ass. The incident reminded her of that time with the Triple C's and Rasheeda screamed like a Banshee. She couldn't go through this again.

A professor came running to her rescue. His secretary Rosa had been walking by on her way to the Black Studies offices on the third floor and ran and got him.

"Professor Temple," the elderly woman shouted. "A female student is being attacked!"

Minutes later, the professor showed up swinging a baseball bat. He managed to break a kneecap. Using his elbow, the rugged professor broke a nose. There probably would have been more damage, but Rosa stepped into the fracas and grabbed his arm. She took the bat from the professor, but not before he had threatened to have the boys expelled. He would've beaten them to a pulp if it wasn't for Rosa.

That was six months ago, and now Rasheeda was a double major in Black studies, but she wasn't willing to give up her businesses dreams. She wanted to create a Black-run financing corporation that would help revitalize small black-owned businesses and support new ones. So she still put up with their whispers. She hated the businesses student wannabes all dressed up in suits like they had somewhere real to be other than a fast-food job, but what could she do? Stripping was a means to an end, just like putting up with these fools.

"R!" Rasheeda heard as she entered the campus that Thursday morning. From the deep bellowing voice, she already knew it was Temple. Even though she was upset about being suspended last night, she still chuckled a bit. She never could believe that that huge echoing voice and boxer body belonged to a White man. Scratch that, a White professor man who walked around with a bat and knew all about the Panthers.

Rasheeda gave Temple a fist bump. "Hey Doc, how's it shaking?"

"Those damn administrative fools are trying to cut my budget again," Temple said almost shouting in anger.

Temple not only helped found Black Studies at Lehman, he had also started the Bronx Oral History project and offered Rasheeda a job working for it, but she had to turn it down. She made at least three times as much stripping.

"No shit. What you gonna do? Take your bat to the meeting?"

"Maybe," Temple said, breaking out in his characteristic belly laugh. That laugh, even at her worst always made her join in, but today she was having trouble even smiling.

"You ok, Rasheeda?"

Rasheeda hung her head. "Work. Moms." Rasheeda was afraid if she said anymore she would cry and then she really wouldn't be able to deal with macro today.

"Look Ra – "

"Don't worry about it Doc, I just gotta get to class."

"Look, I gotta get to this meeting and then go give a talk at Fordham tonight, but come by the office."

"It's ok."

"Rasheeda—I expect to see you in my office tomorrow for lunch."

Rasheeda felt her lip quiver. "A'ight Doc," she said throwing up her fist. "Tomorrow then."

CHAPTER **13**

Khalil looked around carefully as the car stopped in front of his building at 143rd Street.

"Peace out, Doo," he said to his friend. "Score one for the hood."

As he got out of the car, Khalil looked up at the row of fifteen-story red brick buildings that made up the north side of the Patterson Projects. He walked slowly toward his own building, 281 143rd Street, with his head down low, as if he were a beaten-down nigga who couldn't do business in the snow and the wind, giving no sign of the two thousand in cash burning a hole in his pocket. As he approached the door of his building, which hadn't been painted in three years, he nodded at the fourteen-year-old Crips gathered across the street. He was trying to look fierce, hoping that his reputation, and time upstate, would keep them from trying anything foolish—but he kept his hand on his .38 to make sure. Everyone in Patterson knew that the best person to rob was a drug dealer because they were the people in the neighborhood who carried the most cash, but since the snow had cut sales to a trickle, he figured he would get a free pass from these wannabe niggas about to go down the same path he did.

As Khalil unlocked the front door, he heard a voice call out to him from the mailbox area in the lobby of his building.

"H-h-h-h-homeboy, you got anything for me? This b-b-b-b-brother's freezing to death and n-n-needs his medicine."

Khalil looked up to see the shivering figure of Ron "The Fly" Thompson, a Patterson basketball legend from the 60's who was now one of Khalil's best customers.

"Damn, Fly, you know nothing moves in the snow. I'll hook you up tomorrow."

"M-m-m-m-my man, if I don't get my m-m-m-medicine, there may be no tomorrow."

"Ten a.m. tomorrow, Fly. 'Till then just keep drinking tea with lots of sugar. You'll survive."

Khalil shook his head sadly at the tall, frail black man with a cane who stumbled away from him. Thirty years ago, Fly had been a Patterson hero, a six-foot-five-inch dunking machine who led Clinton High School to a city championship and regularly busted up NBA players in the Rucker Tournament, or in the gym at PS 18. He had gotten a scholarship to the University of Iowa, but something happened there with point shaving and Fly returned to the Bronx in disgrace. Once down, he never picked himself up.

Catching dollars in whatever hustle he could find, Fly sought comfort in weed and women until his mind and body failed him and he became the subject of The Bitch Queen Heroin. Now his teeth were falling out, his clothing smelled of urine, and his eight children, fathered with five different mothers, gave him a wide berth. Fly Thompson was a stone junkie, one of hundreds in the Patterson Houses, and a living reminder of what happened to black men of promise in the Bronx if they made a few mistakes.

As Khalil walked to the elevator and almost choked on the smell of urine, the constant tension and frustration he lived with hit him hard. His life was at a dead end—what he did tonight was much easier and more lucrative than selling drugs, but if he ever got caught, it was the end of freedom, as he knew it. Po-po took carjacking very seriously, especially if it involved people with money. Plus, if they could find a crime pattern that was familiar they would put their best detectives on the case and track down the niggas that did it.

His other hustle was much safer, but it never led to big scores. The police and drug dealers had their own little dance going. For the most part, Five-O looked at heroin dealers as people who helped keep the projects calm and only came down on them when some politician filed a complaint. Most of Khalil's clients were beaten, broken-down men and women who mainly harmed themselves. They were regular and reliable, but when he looked into their bloodshot eyes and toothless mouths, Khalil couldn't help seeing himself twenty years later, provided he was still alive. Shit, what he lived with was almost as bad as being in jail.

The elevator door opened and revealed the smiling face of Mrs. Johnson, a heavy-set fifty-year-old woman, partly crippled by arthritis, who lived on the ninth floor. She was the conscience of the Patterson Projects.

"How you doing, boy?"

"Fine, Mrs. Johnson. How are you?"

"I'm always fine when Jesus is with me! And my Savior never leaves me! I'm going to praise him right now! Church starts in half an hour."

"Mrs. Johnson, it's slippery out there. Do you want me to walk you to church?"

"No, Khalil, I have my cane and my Jesus, and they will get me to and from where I need to go. You take care of that mother of yours. She needs your help a lot more than I do."

"Thank you, Mrs. Johnson."

"And boy, stay out of trouble. You're one of the good ones around here. Jesus gave you a loving heart," Mrs. Johnson said, putting her wrinkled but surprisingly soft hands on Khalil's arm.

"I know, Mrs. Johnson, but sometimes it's hard to walk His path."

"Just try, boy, I'll be praying for you," she said, smiling broadly. Looking at the beautiful wrinkles around her eyes, Khalil couldn't help but smile back as he watched her step outside onto the street.

Khalil stepped into the elevator and pressed the button for his floor. He said a silent prayer and heard the motor crank into action. Fortunately, the car reached its destination without any stops and Khalil walked toward his apartment, steeling himself for the depressing scene he knew he would find inside.

CHAPTER **14**

As Khalil walked toward his apartment, the noise came pouring out from 11R, a mixture of television sounds and screams.

"Give me the changer, nigga."

"Bitch, I ain't watching basketball. You know the Knicks ain't shit."

Khalil put the key into the door and walked into the hallway. His niece and nephew, both in diapers ran up to him and grabbed his legs.

"Uncle Khalil, what you got for us?" his three-year-old niece shouted.

"I didn't have time to get you a present, Jalonda, but I've got something for your mom and she'll get it for you tomorrow," Khalil said as he patted his niece's head. Neither released his leg. His niece and nephew clung to him as if he were their one grasp on sanity.

Khalil staggered into the living room with one child on each leg, knowing that the scene he encountered would remind him of the dead-end his life was at—the TV blasting, clothes scattered all over the floor, cheese doodles and chips on the table, his sister and mother in their bathrobes half-naked, zoned out in two tattered arm chairs, while his brothers wrested with the remote on the couch.

Khalil staggered up to his sister and shook her by the shoulders.

"Kameeka, wake up! I've got something for you."

"Go away, Khalil, I'm resting," she replied, not even opening her eyes to meet her younger brother's. Khalil looked down at his baby sister. Like their mother, she had once been not only one of the flyest sisters in the Patterson Houses, but smart too. She had always been at the top of her class until she met the father of her first child, Jesse. Now, Jesse had always been a major player, but for some reason Kameeka thought she could change him. And for a while, it looked like she was right. But then she got pregnant, and Jesse skipped off never to be seen again. Kameeka had never been the same. No matter what Khalil did, he couldn't get her to pick herself back up again. She barely even got dressed anymore and it broke his heart.

"All you do is rest, Kameeka," Khalil yelled, exasperated. "Except when you let some dumb nigga stick his dick in you! Now wake up and take care of these kids. And try to feed them something healthier than cheese doodles."

"Kiss my ass, Khalil," Kameeka said, meeting his gaze. "I don't have to listen to no drug-dealing nigga. You may talk like a preacher, but you peddle death. Now let me go back to my beauty sleep."

Khalil increased the pressure on Kameeka's shoulders until she hollered with pain.

"Nigga, let go of me! I'm gonna kill your ass!" she hollered trying to wrestle free from the increasing pressure.

"Bitch, you had those kids, now you're gon' take care of them. Get up, put those titties in your robe, and start reading to them from those books I got you. And, oh yeah, here's two hundred dollars. Go out and get them some decent clothes and some food that's better than the shit they been eating."

Kameeka grabbed the money and stood up to face Khalil, her right breast now fully exposed.

"Where you get that money, Khalil? You ain't had a real job in three years. And I know ain't nobody buying drugs when it's snowing."

Khalil rolled his eyes. "Kameeka, what do you think? I robbed a bank. Now get up and take care of those kids."

"Okay, okay," Kameeka said as she closed her robe, put the money in her pocket and took her son and daughter from Khalil and put them on her lap. Finally, she snapped out of her stupor and gave Khalil a look filled with a sadness and despair, a look that hit him like a hammer.

"Thanks, Khalil," she said, turning to stroke Jalonda's head. "Sorry for being such a bitch. What you do to get that paper ain't my businesses. I don't know what me and the kids would do without you."

"Word, Kameeka. You and the kids my blood. And blood takes care of blood. But someday, Kameeka, you need to stop messing with those trifling niggas and go back to school. Ain't no future here for you and these kids. You need to start thinkin' bout getting out."

Khalil then turned his attention to his two brothers, Keyshawn and Kenyatta, who had stopped fighting the minute they hear him mention money.

"What you got for us? What you got for us?" they said in unison.

"This your lucky day. I hit the lotto. Each of you get a fifty," Khalil said as he held the money high over his head with both hands. "If you stop fighting and give me a little peace."

"We with you, Khalil, we with you. We need to get paid."

"Well, this money's for you, but the minute I hit the bedroom, I want some privacy. Word?"

"Word," they said.

Khalil dropped his hands and gave each of his brothers a fifty while they ran around the room dancing and screaming. "And remember there's more where this came from if you get A's on your next report card."

Finally, Khalil turned his attention to his mother, passed out on the other chair. She hadn't budged since he came in. He looked at her bloated body and once beautiful face, now disfigured by scars inflicted by violent boyfriends, and lines of worry imposed by years of struggling to take care of her four children with little or no help. She had once been a Patterson House legend, a young sister who made heads turn in the street while she took care of business in the classroom. But she'd been unable to resist the hustling niggas who sweated her everywhere she went, whether it was to school or the corner store, and she finally gave in and got pregnant when she was only fifteen. With little help from a mother who was in and out of rehab, she somehow managed to get a GED and job in the Bureau of Motor Vehicles and took care of Khalil and Kameeka well enough to keep them from going into foster care. Still, she couldn't ever give up her party girl dreams long enough to get out of public housing and stop getting pregnant and now, two more kids later, she was trapped in the same life as her mother before her.

"Ma, wake up!" Khalil yelled in her ear. "I've got the money to pay

Con Ed. I ain't gonna watch these lights get turned off again. The boys need to study."

When his mother didn't react, Khalil slapped her face on both sides, not hard enough to hurt her, but hard enough to get her attention. Her pink bathrobe was frayed at the edges and years of disappointment lined her face.

"Get up, dammit. This ain't right. You got kids in here and you dead drunk."

"Fuck off, Khalil," she said, not even raising her eyes to meet his. "I'm tired. I get no help from anyone. If I want to drink, I'm damn well gonna do it. As long as I keep a roof over your nappy heads, you ain't got nothing to say."

"I got something to say if we got no electricity. This ain't just about you. You got four kids in this house, six if you count me and Kameeka."

Khalil's mother stood up, arranged her bathrobe and marched to the kitchen to serve herself another drink. "Damn right, I have four kids, and you'd all be in group homes and foster care if I didn't drag my ass off to work every Monday. So don't get righteous on me, Khalil. You've given me enough stress to drive any mother to drink. Between the drugs and the fighting, I haven't slept since you started junior high school. If you had just stayed in school and gone to college, maybe we'd be out of here by now."

"Yeah, if I had stayed in school, we'd definitely have been out of here... in a homeless shelter! Here's three hundred dollars for the gas and electric. Don't ask me where I got it." Khalil sighed—he'd been having this same conversation since age fourteen, but no matter how much trouble he got into, he always took care of his.

"What you do boy, rob a bank?"

"Yeah, Ma, that's exactly what I did. I found a cash machine."

"Jesus save us. My boy is a gangsta," she said settling back into her chair and taking a long drink.

"You can call me whatever you want, Ma, but without gangstas like me, half the people in Patterson be out in the street."

Khalil gave his mother the three hundred dollars for the electric bill, then stormed into the bedroom, which he shared with his brothers, slammed the door and lay down on the bed. He had a ferocious headache. From his tiny twin bed, Khalil looked over at his brothers' bunk bed that crowded their already tiny room. Other than a large dresser and small closet there was barely any place to move around. Most of his stuff, Khalil had to store under his bed. Other than a few pictures Rasheeda had given him to tape to his wall, and a Jay-Z poster one of his brother put up, the room was sparingly decorated. They didn't even have a bookshelf or desk for Kenyatta and Keyshawn to study at or leave their schoolwork on. Instead, the few school books they had were piled under their shared bed or strewn around the living room.

Khalil felt like a trapped animal. No matter what he did, he couldn't escape the grind of dealing, or the constant strain of living in an apartment with two broken women and four needy children. The only real joy in his life came from Rasheeda, but how much longer could he keep her in his life with no job, no real future, and no place to take her when they found time to be alone. Here he was, a drug-dealing nigga with a long criminal record, spending time with a college girl. Yeah, she was a hood rat just like him, and she worked in a strip club, but she was going places once she got that degree, and she'd get there without him unless something changed in his life.

Times had been hard for both of them, and he needed to do something to show Rasheeda that he was still her boo, the only brother in the Patterson worthy of her love. He counted the remainder of the money Juno had given him. Fourteen hundred dollars. He was going to give Rasheeda a night to remember, something that would make her keep him in her heart until his luck changed. He took out his cell phone and sent Rasheeda a text message, telling her to meet him at the G Bar tomorrow night at nine thirty so he could present her with the two gifts he had in mind, a diamond necklace and a night at the New York Hilton.

Khalil thought back to the night he met Rasheeda and smiled. He had been taken by his connect to the Strip Club to celebrate a flush time in their business and had been smiling and stuffing bills in the G string of this beautiful, dark-skinned sister whose body was so agile it seemed made of rubber. Something about him must have stirred her, because she bent over, at an impossible angle to rub her mouth on the outline of his dick, which was almost bursting through his pants. He started breathing heavily, afraid he was going to cum right then and there.

"*Cabrón! Dios mio!*" he heard his connect shout. "You're going to get come stains all over those pants."

"Here sister," he said peeling off three hundred dollars from his billfold. "Take him into one of the private rooms and do him right. He's had a good week."

"Follow me," she said, giving his dick one more vibration with her lips, before gracefully vaulting to the floor and taking his hand.

"What's your name, sister?" Khalil asked, as he followed her, hand in hand, toward the back of the club, praying his seed wouldn't burst then and there.

"They call me Fantasy, but my real name is Rasheeda," she said, a hint of sadness in her voice.

"I'm Khalil," he said, noticing that she didn't just give him her stripper name. As they walked through a long hallway, painted black with doorways on each side he couldn't help but think of his sister and mother. "You know you're too young and beautiful to be working here."

"Some of us have bills to pay," she said, leading him into an eight-by-eight windowless room, with a large red sofa chair in the middle, that was bathed blue light. "Now, relax and let me do my job."

CHAPTER **15**

Gently, Rasheeda led Khalil to the red chair and with a smooth motion sat him down, so his back was at a forty-five-degree angle against the tilted leather.

"You know, you're not too bad yourself," she said, removing her G-string top. Khalil gasped at the sight of her full, perfectly formed breasts.

"And there's kindness in your eyes," she continued, "something I don't see around here very often. So I'm going to take my time. Let me take you to a place you haven't been before."

"Sister, I need to go somewhere," Khalil said as she brushed her breasts lightly across his face and moved her hand along the outline of his dick.

As he looked into Rasheeda's beautiful face, he saw a look that he noticed in almost every woman from the hood he knew, a look of resignation that came from constant exposure to pain. But in those subtly slanted eyes, he also saw intelligence and a determination not to let pain define her or beat her down.

He felt his heart go out to her in a way it rarely did with women he met.

"Sister, you need to go somewhere more than I do," Khalil said, as she lowered herself onto his lap and began rotating her hips and butt across his groin. Softly, but firmly, he took hold of her right wrist with one hand and gently stroked her cheek with the other.

"Stand up sister. I'm gonna show you something most brothers around here don't know—that giving is better than receiving."

Khalil put his arms around Rasheeda and lightly ran his lips across her forehead before lifting her off him and placing her in the chair. With a graceful motion, he lowered himself to his knees and put his head between Rasheeda's legs.

"You don't have to do this," Rasheeda said, startled by Khalil's actions.

"Yes I do," Khalil said.

Slowly, he spread her legs apart, and began licking her inner thighs. He soon began moving his tongue and lips along the G string that covered Rasheeda's sex, creating a steady vibrating sensation that went to the core of her being.

"Oh my God, oh my God, oh my God," she cried out. "Don't stop, please don't stop."

Khalil pushed the cloth aside and put his tongue inside Rasheeda, rotating it slowly and moving it with practiced strokes across the little mound on top of her pussy while he pulled her closer to him, both arms holding her lower back.

"Ooh ah! ooh ah! Yes!" Rasheeda screamed as Khalil increased the speed of his tongue's movement. She felt the tension flow out of her, and the world disappear.

"Love me, love me, love me, don't stop, don't stop, Ah yes that's my spot! Baby, I'm coming!" Rasheeda screamed as she shuddered in ecstasy over and over again.

Khalil stayed between Rasheeda's thighs as she started to relax, leaning his head against her mound, gently kissing her thighs. This was the best place in the world. He never wanted to leave it.

Then Rasheeda woke up from her trance.

"Oh my God," she said. "Where did you learn to do that? I've never had a man make me feel that way."

She moved his head up from her legs and looked into his eyes. When Khalil didn't respond, she said, "You are one special brother." Standing up, Rasheeda grabbed his hand, seductively stroking his palm. Then she whispered, "Now let me take care of you."

"You already have," Khalil said, cupping her chin with his palm and raising her gaze to his. "More than you will ever know. But I have to ask you a question. Was this more than business for you? Because if it was, I want to start seeing you outside of this place."

Rasheeda smiled broadly, continuing to caress his hand as she looked into his eyes. "Khalil, this had nothing to do with business. That was Rasheeda you were just with. The other customers, they just see Fantasy, the person I invent for the job."

Khalil put his arms around her and kissed her. "Next week, we get together."

That was one year ago, and Rasheeda had played a few games making him come in to pursue her, or ignoring him when he was at the club, but Khalil didn't mind. He could tell that she had been burned and just needed to feel secure. But once he proved himself, the two were inseparable.

Though it was difficult, given their crowded apartments, to find private space without renting a hotel room, they managed to get a couple of hours alone together. Sometimes it was only once a week. They devoured one another physically, and told each other things they shared with no one else.

Rasheeda saw the loving, vulnerable side of Khalil that he could not reveal on the streets. Khalil saw the fierce intelligence and driving ambition that impelled this beautiful, oft-injured young woman to put herself through college by stripping when there was no other way to pay tuition. Khalil vowed he would rescue her from the clients that preyed on her like sharks, even though he had no means to turn that dream to reality. All he could do was become lost in her beauty, and show her a tenderness so astonishing that she felt God had stepped down, and touched her life with grace.

Once, when Rasheeda asked him how he had learned to lose himself giving a woman pleasure, Khalil revealed the horrible tale of abuse and manipulation that exposed him to the secrets of female sexuality at a tender age.

It had all happened when Khalil was six. His mother had found a new babysitter for him, a woman named Sharon from the building next door who she had gone to high school with. No sooner than his mother had left, than the woman, who was large and powerful and angry-looking said to him,

"Come here, boy. I want to take a good look at you."

Khalil walked over the woman. Sharon lifted him up smothered his lips with hers thrusting her tongue into his mouth.

"Hmm, boy that tastes good. You just like candy. Now let's see what else you've got."

Sharon put him back down on the floor and led him over to the couch, where she sat down and pulled down his pants.

"Damn, boy, you got some size on you," she said, grabbing his dick. "I haven't been with a man in months, and you might just do the trick."

Then she put her mouth on his dick and started sucking greedily.

"Ouch, you're hurting me," Khalil said, surprised by the pressure of her large black lips.

"Damn, boy, if that's pain, what do you think pleasure is?"

As Khalil felt himself hardening, Sharon took her mouth off him, pulled down her skirt, took off her panties, and put Khalil on top of her.

"Now, Momma's gonna give you the ride of your life," she said, trying to put his dick in the dark hair-covered slit between her legs, but the violence of her actions made Khalil sick with fear and his dick went soft, too soft to push through the folds of her skin.

The woman started screaming at him. "Boy, what good are you! You've gone soft on me. Shit, that's a waste of good equipment."

Khalil cowered in fright, expecting the woman to hit him, when a diabolical grin crossed her face.

"Boy," she said, "Your dick might not work, but I bet you're tongue does. Momma's gonna show you something you'll remember for the rest of your life."

As Khalil sat whimpering on the couch, Sharon went over to the refrigerator. She opened the door and said, "Just what the doctor ordered," before returning to Khalil holding a large jar of Welch's grape jelly.

"Boy, I'm gon' show you something that's gon' make you a woman's best friend. Just do what I tell you to do and we both be happy."

Sharon opened the jar, took a huge slab of the purple jelly in her hand, and smeared it over the slit between her legs. Then she sat down on the couch next to Khalil with her legs apart and commanded, "Lick it off." When Khalil hesitated, Sharon drew back her hand and said, "Don't make me hit you." Confused and fearful, Khalil got down on his knees, plunged his head between Sharon's legs and began licking the jelly off.

"Harder, harder, harder," Sharon cried out. "Ooh! You do me soo good! Move that tongue around! Put it in there. Ooh-wee-e-e-e!"

Khalil shook in terror of the huge woman above him, who squirmed with every motion of his tongue. He plunged his lips and mouth deeper into her, trying to forget where he was, trying to disappear.

"Ah, ah-ah-ah-ugh!" Sharon cried out, shaking so uncontrollably that she almost hurt him. "I'm cum-m-m-ing!"

All of a sudden, the tension flowed out of her and she gently moved Khalil's head away from her thighs. Smiling greedily, she took a tissue and wiped the jelly and juices from Khalil's lips.

"Boy, you're a natural at this! I haven't felt this good in months," she said. "When you grow up, the women are gon' love you."

Then, she grabbed Khalil firmly by the back of his head and looked him in the eye. "Boy, you can't tell anyone about this. This is our little secret. It's a special game we play, okay?"

"Okay," Khalil replied. The game went on for the next two years Sharon was his babysitter, once, sometimes twice a week. He felt shame at what he did, but also an odd sense of power at his ability to make a grown woman shake and go weak. And Sharon was right; women did love him when he went down on them and gave them pleasure, but he was always too embarrassed to say where he learned it. Until Rasheeda. With Rasheeda, Khalil could say anything and not fear rejection or condemnation. Somehow, she felt that his essential goodness counted more than any of the terrible things he had been through, or some of the bad things he had done. He had never dreamed that someone like Rasheeda could come into his life and he had to keep her with him, no matter what it took. He had to rescue her from that awful place she was working before something happened to destroy her dreams and crush her pride.

CHAPTER **16**

Khalil lay down on the bed and fell asleep instantly, still in his clothes. He awoke ten hours later and saw the sun creeping through worn-out blinds. That meant it was a business day. He staggered into the cramped and crowded bathroom, found his toothbrush, covered it with paste and brushed carefully. His connect would be out with his packages. Khalil picked up his North Face jacket from the chair, put it on, took his wallet, keys and pager and walked quietly through the living room, trying not to wake Kameeka and her children. If he could get through today, tonight would be special.

Khalil closed the door, walked through the hallway and took the staircase down. He exited the building quickly and began walking slowly on 143rd Street toward Third Avenue, his hands in his pockets and his hood covering his head. Although he appeared to be looking straight ahead, he was always taking quick glances to his right to see what was in the street. When he saw the green Range Rover move slowly toward him, he eased gracefully over the snow bank and entered the open door of the car.

"*Cabrón*, the sun is out. It's a good day to do business," Julio told him, giving him a fist bump.

"What do you have for me, *amigo*?" Khalil asked.

"Fifty packets of Kabull, ten dollars a pack."

"Ten dollars a pack!" Khalil cried. "Bro, that's extortion. You know I can't get more than fifteen dollars on the street. It's a recession."

"Blame your man, Obama, who, *Dios mio*, I voted for. With all those troops going to Afghanistan, the poppy farmers are feeling the heat. The price has doubled."

"Damn, how's a brother goin' to make a living? That means I have to sell twenty packets to make a hundred dollars. I might as well be working at McDonalds."

"I'm sorry, Khalil, but you know how the business goes. Supply and demand."

"Shit, I gotta find a better way to make a living. This ain't worth the trouble."

"Tell me about it. But this is all we have. This is all we know. Niggas like us is expendable. It's drugs, prison or the homeless shelter and I ain't sleepin' on no bench."

"I feel you," Khalil said. "I'll catch you in a few."

Julio opened the door and Khalil got out at 144 Street and Morris Avenue, right next to PS 18 and three blocks from Lincoln Hospital. He walked slowly toward the line of benches that sat near the sandbox and monkey bars on the 3rd Avenue side of the project. It was once built as a playground, but was now the hangout of hustlers and neighborhood junkies. Mothers and children were afraid to go there. A fifty-year-old woman, white-haired and nearly toothless walked up to him.

"Thank God it's you, Khalil. I've got the shakes. I couldn't go another day without."

Khalil handed her a packet as she put fifteen dollars into the pocket of his jacket.

"Bye, Mildred," he said. "You take care of yourself."

One after another, they came by, the beaten and the broken. They were happy to see him, and desperate to fill the aching hole inside them with a drug that made them forget. After four hours, Khalil had one hundred dollars and a desperate headache. He walked back to his apartment, and put away his stash and his gun in the safe he kept under the bed. Then he took some time to think. His mother was at work; his brothers were in school. He even had time to shave and take a shower.

After cleaning himself up, Khalil put on his best-knit shirt and wrapped his gold chain around his neck and looked in the mirror. He liked what he saw enough to smile. He went to the closet and took out the full-length leather coat that he only wore for special occasions. He wanted to look prosperous for Rasheeda. He wanted her to be proud of him. He packed his shaving equipment, his underwear and a change of clothes for the hotel in a small bag he kept in his closet. No one at the hotel would be able to tell he was a dealer. He could be a rapper, a musician, even a professional athlete. He was clean and he was fly, at least on the outside.

Khalil went into the safe and took out the $1,400 dollars he had left from the car theft. Life was hard, but this was going to be a night to remember. It was car service all the way. First, Diamonds five hundred, where he was going to buy Rasheeda her pendant. Then it was off to the G Bar. Khalil top it all off with a night at the New York Hilton accompanied by the only girl he had ever loved. This was what he lived for. It was the only thing that made him feel alive.

CHAPTER **17**

Even with the thousand dollars in her pocket from Wednesday, Rasheeda cursed at herself under her breath. Her momma always said she was an uppity nigga. It would have taken five minutes to give that man a lap dance, Rasheeda thought in despair. With a week off and rent and food to buy for her moms and Junior, there was no way she was going to be able to make enough now to get an extension on her tuition, even if Khalil came through with something. Taking out her cigarettes, Rasheeda sighed. Not that she would ask him anyway—he had his own problems to deal with. Maybe Temple would come up with a way when they met tomorrow but she didn't see how. She would just have to withdraw again for the semester, work hard, save up and go back next year. At this rate, she'd be thirty by the time she finished her school, still stuck in a stupid G-string. The image of a dimpled ass and stretch marks flashed before her eyes—she was gonna end up an old, ugly stripper.

The problem was no one was about to give a loan to a sistah from the projects with an outta-work mother. She couldn't even use the money she made from stripping to catch a break—if she declared that money, most of it would be taken away in taxes and they would still deny her loan. Trudging through the snow, Rasheeda looked at the Kennedy Fried Chicken on one corner, the slimy Chinese on the next, and the men huddled outside the bodega with their brown paper bags. Even with a black man in office, getting outta the ghetto was a joke. The Money Bags were few and far between and even when he did drop serious money, her moms just ended up drinking it up. Like last spring when she got arrested for disorderly conduct, resisting arrest and possession and Rasheeda had to bail her out and spend all her school money on getting a lawyer to make sure her mom didn't go to jail and they didn't lose Junior to foster care. They were still paying off that lawyer. Rasheeda was mostly stuck with the reality that at twenty dollars a pop, it took ten lap dances just to pay for a single credit, even with city tuition.

The sad thing was, Rasheeda had done everything right. She was one of the few girls to stay out of the gangs, turning her focus to school as an escape. And she never got pregnant either, unlike a lot of the girls she grew up with. Something about watching her moms bring home man after man and never seeing them more than once, turned her off from sex. She would watch her mom wait for calls, drinking herself into a depressed stupor. On top of that, Rasheeda already knew as much as she wanted to about raising a child.

With her mom getting knocked up again just two years prior, Rasheeda had become the primary caretaker and breadwinner for the family. She wanted out so bad that when other girls her age thought about the next man, or the next party, she thought about college. Funny thing though—even being the top student that she was, no one ever mentioned applying to college. In fact, when she went to the guidance counselor to send out her transcripts, he looked at her surprised before saying something about how she did have highest SAT scores in the school.

Rasheeda never let any of that stuff get to her, but the lost week of work really brought her down as she walked the last few blocks home in the dirty snow. She remembered when she first got into Lehman for business. She thought she had got the golden ticket outta hell. A few years of hard work and she would be able to get a job on Wall Street, maybe even get her mom some real help, and raise Junior in a real environment. Even when she got denied financial aid because with welfare and two dependents her moms made above the minimum, she didn't worry. Rasheeda couldn't imagine being poorer, but she still didn't let it get to her. She went to bank after bank after bank for a loan. She was sure someone would see her letters of reference and grades and Lehman entrance letter and cut her a break. But she heard the same thing over and over again. She was "too risky," "undesirable," "no collateral." Until finally, she took herself down to a Black-owned bank she heard about. Of course, the crackers would turn her down, but Rasheeda was sure a brother or sister would see her value. Turning the corner toward the Mitchell House, Rasheeda shook her head remembering the Oreo that stared at her breasts for a good ten minutes before denying her application. She would never forget his name, Mr. Robinson, and the way he looked down at her as if he was better than her because he had a nameplate and an expensive suit.

"I'm sorry, Ms. Jones, but I'm afraid at this time we cannot offer you a loan."

"Why the hell not? Did you read the letters? My teachers, my boss. They vouch for me."

"It's just too much of a risk. Most people in your situation don't complete their education."

"Why the hell do you think that is? 'Cuz we ain't got no one to help us! How the fuck am I supposed to finish my education if I can't pay for it?"

"I'm sorry, Ms. Jones, but I'm going to have to ask you to lower your voice."

Rasheeda got up and sauntered over to the desk. Seductively she sat on the edge and gently ran her hand over his face, toying with his ears. Licking her lips, she leaned in so he could get one last look at the perfectly formed breasts he had been drooling over for the ten minutes he was supposedly "assessing" her case.

"No, I'm sorry," she purred.

"Huh?" he said obviously still mesmerized by her open sexuality.

Yanking down hard on his ear, she whispered, "I'm sorry that you seemed to have forgotten not only what it means to be a proud black man, but how to recognize an African Queen when you meet one. I hope you enjoyed looking at my breasts as well as my booty when I saunter out of here, 'cuz all them white women you love so much or try to impress because they make you feel important—not only will they never suck your dick like I could, but every time they try, I hope you know it's just because they get excited over a black man. See what you see in me—the risk—is the *only* thing they want from you."

"Ms. Jones…" he said, standing up.

"Don't worry, I can show myself out."

CHAPTER **18**

Just off the 138th Street stop, Rasheeda stepped over the buckets of strewn garbage, fried chicken wings and Colt 45 bottles as she made the way to her building. That bank incident had been over two years ago and shortly after she started working at Cheetah's. Her moms was right. She was a uppity nigga but she didn't care. If that's what it took to survive...

She wasn't racist and she really didn't believe all that, but it still hurt to be told she wasn't worth the investment, even when she went to her own people for help. She expected it of the white folk, but the brothers, too? Or her sisters at Lehman who still joked behind her back about her stripping? One thing Rasheeda vowed was if she ever made it out and got her degree, she wouldn't forget where she came from. She would start her own bank, but a bank that believed in black people instead of just seeing poverty, failure, and risk.

Rasheeda opened the door of her building, gagging from the strong smell of malt liquor and stale food. Rushing over to find Leroy, her neighbor, passed out on the stairwell again, Rasheeda said to herself, "When, when I get out." It didn't matter how she did it but she was not going to end up like her neighbors, her mother.

"Yo, Leroy, you a'ight?" Rasheeda said, shaking the old man gently. Rasheeda had been helping Leroy get up the stairs for close to a decade.

Leroy cracked his eyes. "R, is that you?" he asked before turning to the side, and vomiting.

At least he didn't vomit on her brand new Gucci's like last time. Well, they had been knock-offs, but still they cost at least two lap dances. Sad. That's the way she measured everything these days. By the number of lap dances it took to buy it.

"Yeah, Leroy, it's me. Let me get you up." Rasheeda sighed, pulling the old man to his feet. Leroy was usually harmless. Like so many of her neighbors he did the worst damage to himself. After being on heroin for the last ten years and crack before that, Leroy was so frail that Rasheeda could practically carry him up the stairs herself.

"I just needs my medicine, but they all out," Leroy said, struggling to pull his head up and form words. These days Leroy was almost without teeth and the lisping only made his deteriorating mind harder to understand.

"I know, Leroy," Rasheeda said, helping him up the last flight to the fifth floor. She didn't even bother to use the elevator anymore. When it worked, it was either an easy way to get raped or robbed and when it didn't, the latest homeless person or addict to get stuck in there would piss everywhere or worse. Rasheeda couldn't stand the smell of piss; the stench of liquor in her own apartment was bad enough.

Standing Leroy up in front of the apartment he shared with his daughter, Kira and her four kids, Rasheeda shook her head. Even when she was younger, Rasheeda remembered that Leroy had been a pretty good-looking cat. His light skin, muscular body and styling Afro turned heads everywhere he went. He could get any girl in the building and in just about any building he hung out around. Now, the rope tied on his dirty army pants barely stayed on his frail body, which was lost in a frayed, no-name blue hoodie. Kira wasn't much better. She and Rasheeda had gone to school together. At least until Kira got pregnant with her first child in the ninth grade and dropped out.

Even through the door, Rasheeda could hear Kira screaming at her kids, all by different men.

"What?" Kira said swinging the door open, her youngest still suckling on her exposed breast.

"Hey, girl. I found him on the stairs, again."

Kira's face softened as she said, "Thanks, R."

Rasheeda stroked the baby's head. "Don't worry about it, girl. You take care."

"You too," Kira said before closing the door.

Taking a deep breath, Rasheeda slumped against the wall, fighting back the tears. Two drops rolled down before she straightened herself back up, slammed her fist into the wall, than let herself into the apartment. Everything would be fine once she talked to Khalil. Not to mention, she was looking forward to their date. She hadn't had a real meal in a while and Khalil always let her order whatever she wanted, in fact, he encouraged it. Dancing as much as she did, it wasn't easy to keep the weight on, and Khalil wanted to make sure her assets were in good shape.

Plus, if everything went well, she would need her stamina for Khalil's pleasure ride. Not that she was worried, but every time she just caught a glimpse of that magic tongue, Rasheeda felt her body shudder. She smiled to herself, just thinking about it. Rasheeda opened up her closet, pushing her worries to the back of her mind. Nothing was gonna change if she let herself have a good time. It would probably help to take a break from her problems.

Rasheeda wanted to look extra fly tonight. Going through her closet, she pulled out a red halter dress she had picked out down on Fordham Road last week after class. Admiring herself in the mirror, Rasheeda looked approvingly at the dress' cut. The fabric fit in all the right places, showing just enough of her full, round breasts and still hugging her petite waist. The clincher was the slit all the way up her thigh. "Yeah, you tight," she said to herself. Quickly, Rasheeda grabbed the DKNY bracelet Khalil bought her for her birthday and the diamond hoops he bought her just because. A beaded clutch purse completed the look and Rasheeda was on her way to a memorable night with her man.

CHAPTER **19**

When Rasheeda stepped into G Bar it was 10 p.m. on the dot, and the place was packed. Rasheeda hated to make her boo wait and he always rewarded her with a car outside her door to pick her up. She caught sight of Khalil right away, sipping on his Hen. As she let the hostess take her coat, she watched as some little ho in a leather mini and cropped top, tried to make a move on her man. Rasheeda could feel her blood start to boil. Oh no she ain't that little sack chasing' ho bout to get a beat down, she thought as she reached to take off her earrings. Just as she started to make her way over to the trick, she caught Khalil's eye. Pointing at Rasheeda, he whispered in the girl's ear and the chic promptly stalked off. Sauntering over, Rasheeda felt the whole room watching her. She knew she looked good and she loved the attention, but it was all for Khalil. She knew it made him look good and that's why she put in the extra care. They could be in sweats and still be all over each other.

Pretending to be mad, Rasheeda stopped a foot away and crossed her arms.

"What was that? You tryin' to play me, boo?"

Khalil broke into a huge grin, playing along. He knew that Rasheeda was more than confident in herself. She didn't worry about hoochies. "Nah, love. I was just schoolin' her you know?"

"I don't know. What you say to her?"

Khalil wrapped his arms around Rasheeda and drew her close. "I told her that why would I even think about messing with a third-rate trick ho, when I had a goddess like you."

"Good answer." Before she could say anything else, Khalil brought his lips down on Rasheeda's, softly massaging her lips with his, before opening her mouth for a deep passionate kiss. Finally coming up for air, Rasheeda felt the tingles reach the tips of her fingers as she stroked Khalil's back.

"Hmm, why we goin' to dinner, boo?" Rasheeda said, licking her lips seductively. "When we can get right to dessert."

Khalil laughed. "Good things come to those who wait. Besides my Queen, we have all night."

"We do?"

"Hmm, after this we going down to the Hilton."

Rasheeda broke out into a huge grin. "Really? Good, 'cuz I'm starvin'!"

"All right, my Queen," Khalil said, nodding to the bartender. "Let's get our table."

Rasheeda barely even thought of her troubles as she and Khalil feasted on all of her favorites: fried calamari and coconut shrimp, for starters, followed by lobster tail and pasta. Khalil always ordered steak or pork chops, but Rasheeda loved her seafood and Khalil loved to see her happy.

Ever since their first date, the couple had been coming to G Bar every few months. Khalil loved to watch the sports on the big screen and Rasheeda loved the upscale atmosphere and live music on Thursdays like tonight, and Saturdays. Rasheeda closed her eyes and swayed to the jazz group as she sipped on her favorite drink, Love Juice, a mix of vanilla and banana rum and pineapple juice. Even though it was just ten blocks from home, the bar felt like a whole different world to Rasheeda. With its exposed brick, hardwood floors and sexy red lighting, Rasheeda felt like she was living the life, not living in public housing nearby. She loved the lit-up bar, red seats and candles—they reminded her of Khalil, urban but elegant, smooth and inviting. He looked good tonight, too, rocking dark jeans and a black knit shirt. A heavy gold chain and full-length leather coat completed the fly look. Rasheeda look up seductively at Khalil and reached her hand across the table, softly massaging his arm.

"Thank you, boo. I needed this."

"You deserve it, and so much more. You hold your family down, go to school and still manage to look so damn fine all the time," Khalil said, scanning the glow of her skin, the fullness of her lips, and finally settling back on her eyes. "Trust me, boo, I know how lucky I am. That's why I would never play you like the cats I see around here."

"I know," Rasheeda said, softly thinking of her own father who ran off, or the men in her building who stayed, like Joe. They were either drug addicts, alcoholics or always running around on their women, or some combination of all the above. They gave black men like Khalil a bad name. "I know," she repeated, looking into Khalil's deep eyes. Khalil was the only man she had ever trusted her heart to. It still scared her a bit, letting those walls down, but deep down, she knew he would hang. He would rather hurt himself than hurt her, and would rather make her happy than take care of himself. He had proven that time after time.

"Go freshin' up, boo, while I take care of this. It's getting' late," Khalil said, interrupting her thoughts.

Rasheeda got up and sauntered over to his side. "What you sayin'? This ain't fresh enough for you?" she said positioning her booty to the best of its advantage.

Khalil opened his mouth, reaching for a quick comeback. Rasheeda knew he enjoyed their lightening-fast banter. Rasheeda could shoot the shit with the best of 'em and even freestyle a bit if the need arose. She had put many a wanna-be-gangasta in their place with her quick wit and ability to think on her feet.

"Hmm, that's what I thought," she said, leaning over and gently kissing Khalil. First, she tugged gently at his bottom lip, before finally bringing her tongue to meet his. As their tongues massaged each other's mouths, she could feel Khalil's hand sneaking its way up her leg, from just above her knee to her upper thigh.

"You better cover yourself with a napkin or somethin'," Rasheeda giggled, noticing the rise of flesh in his lap. "And I better take off before your girlfriend comes back," Rasheeda gave Khalil's chest a squeeze and sauntered off.

CHAPTER **20**

When Rasheeda returned from the bathroom, she had barely approached their table when she saw light bouncing as if a small disco ball had landed on their table.

"Oh my God! Oh my God!" she repeated to herself as she got closer to the table. Slowly, the shape of an "R" in diamonds came into focus. "Oh my God, Khalil!" she squealed, running over to pick up her pendant.

"This is for me? This is mine?" Rasheeda said fingering the necklace.

"Unless you know any other 'R' I should be spending my money on?" Khalil laughed, rubbing her lower back. The "R" was almost the size of her palm, and was studded with diamonds and set on a thick white gold chain.

Still standing by the table, Rasheeda leaned over, speechless—the first time in a long time—and kissed Khalil. Looking back at her necklace, she finally said, "Thank you. This is the nicest thing anybody's ever gotten me."

"Good. I don't like to be shown up," Khalil said as Rasheeda retook her seat. "Well, ain't you gonna model it for me?"

Rasheeda laughed. "Of course. Naked! Now, let's get out of here."

Even in the cab, Rasheeda couldn't keep her eyes off the pendant. She usually loved watching the city lights go by, but this necklace was fly! She couldn't wait to show Erika when she went by to help her with her GED, and she just knew Monica was gonna say how lucky she was again that she *let* her have Khalil. After she picked her jaw off the ground that is. Rasheeda laughed.

"What's so funny, boo?"

"Nothin'. I'm just so happy."

"Good. We're here," Khalil said, handing three twenties to the cab driver. "Keep the change."

Rasheeda looked up at the New York Hilton. She had walked by the imposing white structure and columned drive many times, but had never been inside. As they entered the marble lobby, Rasheeda looked up in awe at the golden hints, the cherry-wood front desk and beautiful flower arrangements.

"Damn, you ain't playin' today, are you?"

Khalil nodded. "Yo, I had to put the room under your name, k?"

"Sure, why? There isn't a warrant out for your arrest or anything, is there? Hold up, your real name isn't, Khalil?" Rasheeda stopped, noticing Khalil's gaze. His eyes were all business and his jaw was clenched.

"It's just that they need a credit card to get the room."

"Okay, okay, that's no problem," Rasheeda said, stroking his arm. "Let's go check out our digs."

"I got cash for you. I'm a give it to you today for the room."

"I know, love. My man always looks out for me, only the best," Rasheeda said soothingly. She knew that the credit-card business was a sore point for Khalil. He hated that he could never get one, just because he never had an income to report. Plus, he didn't want to have a trail of cash deposits in a bank account just to have some cracker come and ask him questions about where it all came from. His savings consisted of a lock box under his bed.

Rasheeda could tell that Khalil was still sore about it when they got to their room, but she knew it would pass. Khalil's bad moods never lasted too long. Instead, she just appreciated all that her man had given her today. She sighed blissfully as she took in the king-size room, huge flat screen and full bath. Rasheeda had never had a bathtub of her own.

"We definitely gonna be soaking in that later," she said, picking up complimentary shampoo and lotion. Leaving Khalil splayed out on the bed, watching the highlights, Rasheeda went into the bathroom, removing every article of clothing and folding them gently on the toilet seat. She stared at her naked body, turning from side to side, inspecting herself for any imperfections.

"Hmm, you lookin' good," she said, pleased with her slender waist, full breasts and booty, and recent bikini wax. All her dancing recently had given her a nice tone on her arms and legs. Finally, she took out the pendent and put it on. The length of the chain was perfect—the feet of the "R" rested ever so slightly on the tops of her breasts.

Five minutes later, Rasheeda sauntered out of the bathroom, placing herself directly in front of the TV. She was sure Khalil wouldn't mind.

"So, what do you think? It look good?"

Khalil sat up fast, licking his lips. "It looks more than good. Damn, girl. That body was meant to wear nothing but a necklace."

"Hmm," Rasheeda said, wrapping her legs around his waist. "I love you, Khalil." She kissed him passionately. Khalil squeezed her tight, and felt the fullness of her breasts swelling against his chest. He stroked her taunt, smooth back.

"I love you, too, my Queen. Let me show you how much," he said picking Rasheeda up and placing her on her back.

"You don't have to. You've already done so much for me today... So much."

Khalil sucked on her left breast, leaving it erect. Smiling, he said, "Girl, how long we gonna be together befo' you realize that I'm not like other men."

"I know, I'm just saying. Hmm-m-m," Rasheeda moaned as Khalil went to work on the other breast.

"Baby, I love seeing you cum, just like I love seeing your big ol' smile when I give you something. I'm happy when you happy."

"Hmm-m-m okay," Rasheeda said. "If you insist."

"I do," Khalil said, working his way down her body. Methodically, he nibbled at her hips, her inner thigh, kissing her everywhere except where her body screamed for most. Next, he spread her legs and massaged the walls of her vagina.

"Damn, girl."

"Hmm-m-m-m."

"It really is a thing of beauty," he said, before slowly licking the fleshy folds.

"You're soo wet."

Rasheeda pressed her hands against the bed board, stretching out her body to its max and focusing on the tingles spreading from her ears to the tips of her toes. Khalil's pace quickened as he moved his tongue in faster and faster circles before beginning to suck on her clit. He wanted to make her beg for it, so he teased her, flicking the hard tip of his tongue over her gently swelling clit. Underneath his hands, her body rose, arching, aching for more. Rasheeda brought her hands down, massaging her own breasts.

"Oh, baby!" Rasheeda gasped, hardly able to breathe. Rasheeda wasn't sure if her body was hot or cold, all she could feel were the tingles everywhere, but now the tingles were electric currents, racing up and down her body.

"Please, please, I can't, hmm-hmm, I can't."

Finally, Khalil returned to her spot, giving in to her needs. Rasheeda shot up, taking in the waves of orgasm over her body before collapsing back onto the bed.

Then, Rasheeda laughed.

"What's so funny now?"

Rasheeda lifted her arm, and felt it shaking uncontrollably. "Damn, look at what you did this time. You've given me the shakes."

Khalil laughed too, as he held her naked body.

Rasheeda turned to him. "Why you still got your clothes on?" She didn't wait for an answer pulling off his shoes, socks and pants. Meanwhile, Khalil had removed his chain and shirt. For a moment, they stopped, staring at each other's bodies before Rasheeda wrapped her legs around him again, riding his already-erect penis. Khalil picked her up and placed her on the stand by the television. They didn't stop kissing once as they clawed each other's backs, enjoying every moment of pleasure.

By four a.m. when Rasheeda was soaking in the bath, they had tried the bed again, as well as the table, and floor, even though it gave Khalil rug burns. As Khalil sat on the toilet sampling the mini bar, Rasheeda looked up at him dreamily. If only it could be like this all the time. She thought about her suspension from work, and wondered how could life be so good sometimes and so damn hard other times?

CHAPTER **21**

Watching Rasheeda soak in the tub, Khalil noticed the dreamy look on her face start to fade.

"Boo, what's wrong?" Khalil asked seeing Rasheeda's face darken for the first time in the evening. "I told you—I know you did fine on your test today. You always trip then get an A."

Rasheeda shook her head. "No," she mumbled.

"An A- then. Still good." Noticing the worry increase on Rasheeda's usually line-free face, Khalil stopped joking. "What's up boo? You can tell me anything."

Rasheeda was silent. "Nothin', I just think I'm gonna have to drop out again this semester."

"What? Why?"

"I can't pay my tuition. I can't get a loan, and I can't even work to try to get the money. They gonna kick me out if I don't withdraw anyways."

"But I thought Money Bags was droppin' big money all the time. Didn't you say the other day that he was your education benefactor?"

Rasheeda sunk deeper into the tub. "He was, but I got suspended. I can't work for a week."

"You kiddin' me, boo?" Khalil clenched his fists.

"No. I was getting ready to leave and some customer, not one of my regulars, grabs me and tries to make me give him a lap dance. It wasn't a big deal, but I don't have to do nothing for nobody, you know? We already have to pay just to work and I didn't feel like it. I told him No and he grabbed me, so I told him to step off and then Ray got all up in my grill 'cuz he's a regular. I didn't know him, but still. I just didn't feel like dancing anymore. My time was up. And so Ray told me to take the week off. The whole week. I really needed to be workin' every day this week to try and put a couple G's down and get an extension on my tuition. You know how all the money I saved off last semester went to my moms."

Rasheeda could feel the anger and tears and frustration welling up inside. She didn't want to burden Khalil with her problems but she could feel the tears coming and she knew Khalil couldn't bear to see her cry. So she slid her head underneath the water, trying to let her tears out beneath the bubbles. When she surfaced, Khalil was deep in thought.

"Look, I can give you $500 tonight. I'll get some more this week and then you go back to work and everything will be fine. We gonna make it through this semester."

Rasheeda smiled trying to hide her desperation. She leaned her head against the bathtub sobbing. Khalil rushed to her side, kneeling by the tub.

"Boo, what's wrong? Why are you cryin'?" Rasheeda sobbed harder. "Why you crying?" She sobbed for five straight minutes, something she had never done, ever in her life. Finally, she turned to meet Khalil's concerned eyes.

"I just can't do it anymore."

"What?"

"Work at Cheetah's."

"Did something else happen, boo?"

"No, it's just the strippin'. I can't stand it anymore. I hate to have all those men even look at my body, the body that's supposed to be only for you. And then, having to touch them," Rasheeda said, her voice cracking. She slammed her fist down in the water. "And then them staring at me at school, the boys laughing and the girls pointing. Even Money Bags makes fun of me and I can't say a thing because I need his money. I feel like a whore, Khalil."

"Okay, okay" Khalil said softly. "You find something else."

"What the fuck else am I supposed to do? You know there's nothing else, not if I want to stay in school. It's three thousand dollars a semester, plus fees plus my moms' business. I can't get out from under."

"You quit then, Rasheeda. I'll take care of things from now on."

"No, Khalil. I'm not gonna watch you go down that path."

"R—"

"No! No crack and no more boosting cars."

"Rasheeda just let me take care of things."

"No! No Khalil. What good are you gon' be to me in jail? You know in that biz it's only a matter of time and with your record, this time it'll be for life!"

Khalil looked down, infuriated by his inability to provide for his woman. Rasheeda saw the embarrassment in his face and grabbed his hand.

"I'm sorry. It's really not so bad. I just had a bad day, okay." Khalil looked into her swollen eyes and nodded sadly. They both knew it wasn't just a bad day. It was a nightmare of a life.

"It's just pretending to like Money Bags and feeling those hands on my body. It grosses me out sometimes. That's all. It's just not fair that he has all that money and I gotta work so hard just to get a little of it." Khalil still didn't say anything.

Rasheeda turned the water on, adding more hot water to her bath. "Imagine if we turned the tables on him somehow, hit 'em back. Like kidnapped him and blackmailed his family for the money. Imagine me goin' up to his rich bitch wife on Park Ave and telling her she had to give *me* money. That would be crazy. I'd take her fur coat too, right off her fancy white back just for good measure." Trying to lighten the mood, Rasheeda laughed, smiling up at Khalil through her tears.

Khalil finally looked up. "That's it, R."

"What's it?"

"That's how we gonna get out. I don't want my girl strippin' anymore, but you right, how else you gonna pay for school? That's how."

"Khalil," Rasheeda laughed tilting her head. "You *loco.*"

"Listen, R," Khalil said taking another sip of cognac. "You know just as well as me that as hard as we tryin', we not gettin' anywhere. Somethin' always comes up— somethin' always goes bad. We gonna end up like our moms pretty soon unless we get out, but to get out we gotta think big."

"Khalil, we ain't gonna kidnap someone." Rasheeda had just been mouthing off. She'd never expected him to take her seriously.

"But we could. It would be easy. We could grab him from your work, then all we gotta do is stash him for a bit, contact the family—wham bam, our lives are set."

"Yeah, until Money Bags goes to the police and we go to jail."

"Well, you know we could…"

"Khalil, I'm *not* going to kill anyone and I don't want you to, either. I already gotta live with what I did when I was younger."

"That wasn't your fault, R."

"I know, but I have that one on me, always. I don't need that on you."

Khalil sighed, thinking about how tough Rasheeda had to be so young. Just imagining her killing that son of a bitch. The thought put ice in his veins.

"Then, we'll move. Go to Mexico or Canada or overseas. With that kinda cash we could go anywhere, do anything. Imagine it, we'd finally be free. Outta the ghetto. Never look back. Start new lives where the apartments are clean, the elevators work and there's not a junkie passed out on any floor."

"I don't know."

Khalil turned, kneeling before Rasheeda almost as if in prayer. "R, think about it. R, we could do this. We could get out."

Rasheeda thought about Mac grabbing her arm, about Mr. Robinson examining her breasts and then denying her loan. She thought about the time when one of her professors turned up at Cheetah's and how she had to dodge his come-ons for the rest of the semester. That had been easy compared to her classmates' daily assaults. Finally, she thought of Money Bag's cold white hands touching her breasts after he made fun of her to those Wall Street bastards who hardly tipped her anyway. She was done having men touch her body like she didn't have a mind. Rasheeda stood up in the bath. Taking Khalil's hands she raised him to his feet and kissed him softly.

"Let's do it."

"For real?"

"For real. Let's get the scumbag's money and get the hell outta here."

Khalil pulled Rasheeda out of the tub, getting half a bath in the process. Whipping the bubbles from his cheek, Rasheeda giggled, imagining their new life.

"I want to feel you inside me," she whispered in his ear.

Khalil didn't waste a moment. Laying her down on the bathmat, he entered her then and there, thrusting to the dream of a new life.

CHAPTER **22**

That Friday morning, Khalil awoke with his mind abuzz. Here he was in the closest thing to heaven he had known in his twenty-two years. The king-sized bed with soft sheets that was twice the size of the one he slept on, the velvet floor-to-ceiling curtains, the artwork all over the walls, the black marble and metal bar with bottles of Courvoisier and Hennessey, the bathtub large enough to hold two people and above all the beautiful, coal-skinned girl lying next to him in bed, her face so peaceful, as though she didn't have a worry in the world.

Khalil wanted to freeze this moment in time, to stay where he was forever. But the clock on the night table said ten and they had to be out of the room by eleven, to return to a life that had them feeling desperate and trapped.

For Khalil and Rasheeda, their whole evening had been a tantalizing taste of a wealth and luxury that some people took for granted. It was also an evening they had only been given because Khalil had been willing to risk ten years of prison by hijacking a car. Now, Khalil and Rasheeda were on a path that could put them in prison for the rest of their lives. He felt bad about possibly leaving his brothers and sister behind, but he would always take care of them, probably better than he could now. Khalil felt nervous, as he did every time he did business on the street, but he was surprisingly unafraid. After all, what did he and Rasheeda have to lose? Their "freedom" was little better than a lifelong jail sentence. Khalil thought of the lyrics from the rap group Dead Prez, which Brother Akbaar had introduced to him in prison upstate.

You don't have to be in jail
to be in prison
Look how we living
Thirty thousand niggas up in the bing,
standard routine
They put us in a box,
just like our life on the block
Behind enemy lines

"Shit," Khalil mumbled. "One jail is the same as another." If it took kidnapping Rasheeda's client and holding him for ransom to get them out of this life for good, it was worth the risk. He just had to make sure his mind was clear, his plan was well thought out, and his boys Doo and Juno were willing to go along.

Khalil felt he was becoming teary eyed. "Boo, you deserve better," he whispered to Rasheeda, as he stroked her cheek. As she opened her eyes, he felt torn between tenderness and steely determination.

"Good morning," Rasheeda whispered softly, stretching her arms high above her head. "You have given me the best morning of my life." She pulled him down to her, kissed him and hugged him so close he could feel her heart beating.

"Just hold me for a few minutes, Khalil," she said, "I want to remember us just this way, together and at peace."

On the car service ride back to the Bronx, Khalil and Rasheeda held each other silently, more and more dejected as the scene outside the window shifted from skyscrapers and luxury apartments to industrial buildings, bodegas and housing projects. The snow on the streets of Harlem and the Bronx was now a gray slush, causing cars to splash pedestrians every time they went through a puddle. People walked slowly and warily, as if resigned to getting soaked by cars or hit by snowballs. When the cab stopped in front of the Mitchell Houses, Rasheeda looked defeated.

Khalil took her face in his hands, kissed her softly and said, "Boo, this is going to work out. I am going to take you out of here. I'll be in touch as soon as I have a plan." He held the piece of paper on which Rasheeda had written down Money Bags' full name, Robert Seidman. He and Doo were going to have to do some research on him before they could figure out all the details. He opened the door for Rasheeda and smiled as she got out.

"Think of this as the first day of our new life," he said before kissing her good-bye.

Khalil spent the next day on the street, making sure his regular clients got their fix. From ten a.m. to seven p.m. he moved around the Patterson Houses, meeting clients in hallways and stairwells, in the still snow-covered playground, and outside Jose's bodega. Police cars passed him by regularly, but never bothered to stop and frisk him, probably since the heroin trade, unlike crack, didn't generate enough revenue to produce worthwhile bribes.

"Five-O was sure right about that," Khalil muttered. He cleared only $120 in a nine-hour day, better than what he would have gotten working in McDonalds, but less than if he got a job with UPS, which of course he couldn't because of his criminal record. Now, he had a chance to put an end to this once and for all. If the kidnapping worked, Rasheeda and Khalil could leave the Bronx forever and start a new life, with a new identity, in a suburb or small town. If it didn't work, his new life would be in Greenhaven or Coxsackie prisons. Either way, he wouldn't have to look into the bloodshot eyes of clients and get a window into his own future.

CHAPTER **23**

A day later, his mind clear, his determination restored, Khalil called Doo on his cell.

"What's up, my nigga?" Khalil said, watching his turf to make sure the Mexicans hadn't returned.

"The usual—school and the store. I don't know how much longer we can keep the businesses going with the rent these thieves are charging."

"I may have a way out, but first I need you to get everything you can find on Rasheeda's biggest client, Robert Seidman."

"What you need to know?"

"Everything. How he makes his money, what he's worth, where

he lives, where his wife shops, where his kids go to school, everything and anything someone would want to know who wants to do business with him."

"Nigga, what kind of shit are you into? This sounds way out of your league."

"The problem with you Africans is that you're always thinking too small. Just get me the information and then we'll talk."

Khalil hung up the phone and went to the coffee shop on 138th and 3rd to warm up. The owner, Milton, who used to be tight with his mother, let him sit there for hours with just a cup of coffee and a piece of pie if business was slow. Two hours later, the cell phone rang.

"Damn, nigga, Robert Seidman is one of the biggest playas on Wall Street. He has 80 billion in a private investment firm that has all the top real-estate people in the city as clients, owns a co-op on Park Avenue, and houses in East Hampton, Palm Beach and Aspen. He has memberships at five golf clubs and is on the Carnegie Hall and Metropolitan Museum of Art boards. And you say this motherfucker goes to a strip club in the South Bronx? What's wrong with him?"

"How the fuck should I know? Maybe he likes pretending he's a thug. Maybe he's got a thing for black pussy. All I know is that he's crazy about Rasheeda, and comes up to get a lap dance from her at least once a week."

"So how does that help us?"

"That's something we need to talk about in person. Where are you now?"

"I'm at the store. Why don't you come up and we can talk in the back room. There isn't enough money coming in and out of here for anyone to put in a wire."

"Word. I'll see you in about twenty."

Khalil called a car to Milton's Coffee Shop and took the ten-minute ride up the Concourse to 165th and Morris Avenue, where a small store with the sign "African Market" stood near the southwest corner. As Khalil walked through the entrance, he found himself in a different world. He saw shelves packed to the brim with fifty-pound bags of rice, huge bins of what looked like yams, but were twice the size, and giant cans filled with okra, beans and tomatoes. A huge man in a full-length yellow robe and matching skull cap, was speaking to several customers in a strange language while Doo, dressed in a sweatshirt and jeans, went to the refrigerator in the back and came out with body parts that Khalil would have never dreamed of eating, presumably from a cow or a sheep.

"Hello, Mamadou. Hello, Mr. Diallo," Khalil said.

"A salaam alaikum," Mr. Diallo replied. "How are you today?"

"A salaam alaikum, Mr. Diallo," Khalil answered." I'm fine. I need to speak to Mamadou for a few minutes about an important matter. I am thinking about joining him at Hostos College."

"Allah be praised," Mr. Diallo said, raising his hands in the air. "That is good news indeed. Please go to the back of the store. I can handle the rest of the customers myself for the next few minutes."

Khalil joined Mamadou in the back of the store where they entered a five-by-five cubicle piled up with bills and receipts, some in English, some in other languages. Somehow they still found room for a computer, a fax machine and a phone.

As Khalil entered, Doo nodded and said, "So my brother, what did you have in mind?"

"A'ight, Doo, here's my plan. It's not that much harder than what we did last week. All we need is a car and a place to take Seidman. Juno can give us both. When Rasheeda goes back to Cheetah's next week, Seidman is going to want to have a lap dance in one of the private rooms. She's going to book it for him, in the room closest to the back door."

"You're sure she's down with this?"

"We both down with this. One way or another, this is going to be the last dance she gives. She goin' to play it like she can't wait to see him. She's goin' to book him for the Cheetah Club Full Service treatment, a full hour in a private room."

Doo nodded, well aware of what could happen during "full service treatment." "When Rasheeda gives you the full treatment, even an old motherfucker like Seidman is going to cum two or three times. But while he's wildin' out, Rasheeda will be spiking his drink and when he starts nodding, she gonna text us. We'll come in through the back door, which will be unlocked, and take him to the car. Rasheeda joins us and we drive over to Juno's and call his wife. Then the fun begins. We gonna be asking ten million dollars ransom."

Doo nodded again. "What's my cut?"

"Twenty percent—two million dollars. Same for Juno. That sound fair to you, Doo?"

"Damn," Doo said, his eyes widening. "With two million dollars, I can buy this store for my father, put my brothers and sisters through college, and have enough left over to build three new houses for our family in Mali. If Juno is in, I'm down."

"Cool. Then let's go see Juno."

CHAPTER **24**

As Khalil waited to meet Mamadou at Jimmy's Luncheonette, one of the last remaining soul food spots in the Bronx, and a place where the partners could get some privacy while making plans, he thought of the time he first realized his friend may have been more dangerous than he was.

It had been a little more than a year ago, early afternoon on a cold autumn day just after Khalil had met his customers.

His cell rang and Doo's voice came up. His usual joking manner was absent. His voice was soft, serious, as if someone had died.

"Salaam alaikum, Khalil. There is something I have to do for my father and I need your help. Some worthless niggas need to be taught a lesson."

"Anything for you, Doo, what's up?" Khalil asked.

"There's been some Claremont niggas fucking with people outside our mosque, beating up the men, pulling head scarves off the women, throwing rocks through the windows and pissing on the door. They say they are tired of Africans coming to the Bronx and taking over their neighborhoods. If we don't leave, they say, they will burn the mosque and start raping our mothers and sisters."

"Damn," Khalil said, "That's some foul shit."

"Yeah, and I'm going to put a stop to it once and for all." Doo said. "You down for this, Khalil?"

Without hesitation, Khalil patted the .38 in his pants "Hell, yes. You know I'm always down to teach a few muthafuckas some respect."

Khalil arranged to meet Mamadou outside his father's store and after paying their respects to Mr. Diallo, the two began walking east on 165th Street toward the mosque. With the snow almost gone, they passed through a crowd of mothers with strollers, some clearly African, others Mexican, Dominican and Puerto Rican, along with hundreds of school children of all ages. Some of the kids were in uniforms, others wore baggy clothes and projected an aura of toughness designed to ward off attack. Although the faces of the people came in a many colors, almost none of them were white, and very few were African American. This was an immigrant neighborhood and the languages on the street were a mixture of English, Spanglish, French, Wolof and Twi, mingled with the hip-hop infused speech of the young. This was a different world than the Patterson Houses, Khalil thought. These people had hope, they moved with a purpose.

Just give them a few years, Khalil had thought to himself. The Bronx will beat them down just like it did me.

When they got to Teller Avenue, they made a left and walked toward 167th Street, where the mosque was located. As they were walking, Mamadou sent a text and soon two muscular dark-skinned young men wearing hooded sweatshirts joined them.

"Youssou, Mokobe, assalaam alaikum," Mamadou said, "This is Khalil. He's here to help us. You all ready?"

The heavier of the two men, the one called Mokobe, pointed to a huge shiny blade at his waist. It looked more like a machete than a knife. The other tapped his pocket as if he held a gun. "We ready," they both said.

The four men turned left on 167th Street and with a nod from Mamadou, began standing in front of a bodega on the southwest side of the street. Directly across from them was a large storefront with Arabic lettering that meant "Islamic Center." As they waited, it seemed like twenty or thirty young people from kindergarten to their teens began assembling on the sidewalk in front of the mosque. The boys were all neatly dressed; the girls were all wearing long dresses and headscarves. They were preparing to go to an after-school program at the mosque where they would study the Qu'ran and learn the Arabic language.

Suddenly, ten young men who looked like junior-high and high school students, all wearing dark hooded jackets or sweatshirts approached them. The boys came charging around the corner from Teller Avenue, screaming and cursing before leaping on the young people in front of the mosque. Viciously, they threw the boys to the ground kicking them, before grabbing the girls and pulling off their headscarves.

"Fuck, Allah. Go back to Africa. Die terrorist die!" they cried as they beat the defenseless school children, throwing one through the window of the Islamic Center. The window shattered on impact, leaving broken glass all over the sidewalk. Then the unthinkable happened. The largest of the attackers, who was almost as big as Khalil, grabbed one of the oldest of the Muslim girls, pushed her against the brick wall of the building next to the mosque, and after pulling off her coat and headscarf, began ripping her blouse and fondling her breasts as he rubbed his groin against hers.

"Now!" shouted Mamadou. The four young men ran across the street, two with guns, two with machetes. As Khalil and Youssou fired shots in the air, Mamadou screamed "Let them go, niggas, or all you gon' die!"

When one of the attackers started running toward the avenue, Youssou shot him in the leg and he crumpled onto the sidewalk, screaming, while the others retreated toward the mosque with their hands up. Meanwhile, Mamadou leaped on the man who was molesting the Muslim sister and sliced off his left ear with one smooth stroke of his blade.

As the man screamed hysterically and blood spilled all over, Mamadou said to the terrified young woman, "Go inside and help take care of the younger ones. Don't call the police for another half hour. We have some unfinished business to take care of."

Nodding, the young woman quickly entered the center. Mamadou grabbed the bleeding, screaming man and marched him into the alley of a building two doors down.

"Bring the other niggas with you!" he shouted to Khalil and his two friends, who had the eight young men line up against the wall with their hands over their head. They left the one who had been shot lying screaming and bleeding on the sidewalk.

"Move muthafuckas!" shouted Khalil, with his gun out as Mokobe and Youssou marched the terrified teens into the alley. Surrounded by garbage and brick walls, Mamadou held the young man on the ground. The boy was screaming as Mamadou pressed his knee pressed hard against his stomach.

"Line these bitches against the wall so they can see what people in my country do to men who come into their village and try to rape their women," Mamadou said. As the eight young men, now shaking with fear stood against the wall, Mamadou shouted, "Mokobe, pull down this nigga's pants."

While Youssou and Khalil kept their guns pointed at the eight wide-eyed young men, Youssou came over to the bleeding man and pulled his pants down, exposing his dick and balls to the cold winter air.

"You tell everyone in Claremont, you touch a Muslim or African woman, this is what happens!" Mamadou screamed, pulling the man's dick roughly away from his balls with his left hand while bringing his knife down with the right hand in a sudden motion, yielding a blood-curdling scream, more horrible than anyone there had ever heard. His knife still upraised, he took the bloody mass that had fallen to the ground and shoved it into the man's mouth.

By now, all the young men against the wall were screaming, and crying. Some were soiling their pants. One vomited. Even Khalil with all the violence and shootings he had seen in his life, felt his stomach turn.

"Run, niggas! Run!" Mamadou shouted ferociously. "And don't look back! And when you get there, tell everyone what happens to people who disrespect our people and our religion."

As the young men ran screaming from the alley, Khalil, Mamadou and their friends calmly put their weapons away and began walking up 167th Street toward the Grand Concourse, leaving the castrated victim screaming on the sidewalk and the other bleeding and choking in the alley.

"Thank you, brothers," Mamadou said. "That's the last time anyone will bother people from our mosque."

Now, a year later at the luncheonette, which was only four blocks from the mosque where Mamadou's family worshiped, Khalil reminded his friend of what they had done together a year before. Mamadou had been right, Khalil thought. That was the last time any project niggas had dared go near a mosque, much less fuck with a sister with a headscarf.

"Damn, Doo. I knew you were rough, but I ain't never seen shit like before. I didn't know you had it in you."

"Listen to this, Khalil," Doo said, pulling out his iPod and turning on a song that had rhymes flowing over a funky horn section. "This is my man, K'Naan. People see Africans in their neighborhood and think we soft, but we've seen shit they can't even imagine. Preach K'Naan."

Let me introduce me
I'm Africa's rap Bruce Lee
Plus they've been trying to shoot me
Since I've been two feet
Where I am from they will pull your card mister
You ain't hard mister
I was initiated at age thirteen and it wasn't a Bar Mitzvah
I'll break a bottle on you like a bad bartender
Let my style venture out
I've got war in me, so let me vent it out
Fela, take me out!

The beats of Fela Kuti kicked in and Khalil looked at Doo in silence, with respect, and a touch of fear. Now that someone else needed to be taught a lesson, someone rich and powerful, Khalil figured he had the right man for the job.

As the waitress brought them the Jimmy's Luncheonette Special—eggs, grits and fried whiting—Doo described for the first time some of the terrors he had seen as a small boy. Khalil had always known that Doo's family had left because of civil war there, but even what he imagined wasn't as horrible as what happened. Doo described the powerlessness he felt, for example, when he watched his ten-year-old sister gang raped. That's why, now in the Bronx, there was no way he was gonna stand by and watch history repeat itself. No one was gonna fuck with another Muslim sister while he watched.

As Doo finished his story, Khalil nodded in agreement. That's how he felt about Rasheeda—he never wanted to see her hurt, depressed or degraded again. His thoughts returned to the kidnapping plan and how perhaps, at least they could both do something to help the people they loved. They wouldn't be powerless anymore.

"That's some heavy shirt, bro. Damn. But now let's see Juno and see how we can get our piece of the pie," Khalil said.

Mamadou picked up his cell and called Juno. "Is this a good time to do business?" he asked. "Good. We have something you're going to like. We'll be there in a few."

As yellow cabs avoided the Bronx, Khalil called a car service and the two men left the coffee shop ten minutes later. They rode to Juno's garage in silence, Khalil still shaken by what he had heard and Doo lost in his own thoughts, his dark face a mask hiding feelings that Khalil could only guess at.

CHAPTER **25**

Less then ten minutes later, the two found themselves silently watching the buildings pass as the car crawled through streets packed with buses, trucks and pedestrians until the driver reached the Bruckner Expressway and turned left under the highway. Since many families lived doubled and tripled up in the South Bronx's apartment buildings traffic could be worse than in Manhattan. The one exception was Hunts Point, where the garages, warehouses and body shops outnumbered the buildings. The car finally began moving quickly when it turned onto Hunts Point Avenue, reaching Juno's garage in less than five minutes.

Khalil and Doo walked through the entrance and headed into Juno's office, where Juno sat amidst a clutter of papers, auto parts and pinup photos, from English and Spanish magazines. Juno's Garafuna community migrated to the Bronx from a predominantly Black region of Honduras that had a different music and culture from the rest of that country. Like many Bronx residents, he looked Black, but spoke Spanish. And like many other Bronx residents, he had seen things in his home country that had scarred him for life and had given him a look on his face that said to anyone with even a bit of street smarts, "Don't fuck with me!"

Juno directed Khalil and Doo to sit on two chairs on the other side of his desk and then looked them over carefully, a shrewd expression on his face.

"So, *mis amigos*, what do you have for me? What's so important that you have to rush to see me in the middle of the day?"

"How would you like to make two millions dollars?" Khalil asked, getting right to the point.

"Hah, hah, that's funny. You two jump up and down when I give you two thousand dollars. Where are you going to find millions? This is the South Bronx, not Wall Street."

"You're right, Juno, but sometimes, Wall Street comes to the South Bronx."

Juno sat back in his chair, intrigued. "*Bueno, dimelo.*"

"I happen to know for a fact that Robert Seidman, a Wall Street investor worth hundreds of millions of dollars is a regular at Cheetah's, the big strip club just off the Grand Concourse. We're going to kidnap him for ransom."

Juno laughed, almost choking. "How the fuck you gonna do that?"

Khalil looked over at Doo, who nodded. Meeting Juno's gaze, he said confidently, "This old white motherfucker is crazy for the Black skin. We got an inside girl there he goes to see three, four times a week. She can't stand him, so she's been putting off seeing him, but next week she is going to agree to give him an hour in a private room." As Khalil continued, he felt an odd mixture of rage and excitement pounding though his chest. "While he's in there busting a nut, she's going to spike his drink, and when he's out, she'll signal us and we'll come in the back door, take him to a private place and hold him for ransom."

"And where do I come in?" Juno said, his face still blank and expressionless.   "You're going to supply the car and the place." Khalil said, with growing confidence.

"And why should I do this?" Juno said, rocking back in his chairs, his arms crossed.

"Because you're going to make more money in two days than you could in ten years. We are going to ask for a ransom payment of ten million dollars. Doo has done research on this guy. He's soo rich that ten million won't make a blip on his bank account. His wife gonna give it up as soon as she finds out her husband's life is on the line. Your cut is two million. Doo's cut is two million. My girl and I will take the other six million, and make a new life for ourselves somewhere out of the city."

"Doo, is this for real?"

"Juno, I go to college to study business and everyone I've spoken to says this guy is a Wall Street legend. While almost every other investment trust is going down the tubes, this motherfucker is still paying ten percent interest on his accounts. This guy is the biggest of the big! You need five million dollars to even open an account with him. And he crazy for our girl!! That's the hook. There's a risk here, but no more of a risk than hijacking a car.

No one needs to get hurt. We take the guy, treat him well, get the money from his wife, and let him go after reminding him that if he goes to the police, we will take out his grandkids. He loves his grandchildren! He won't make any problems."

Juno got up and walked over to the window, hesitating for about thirty seconds, before turning to face the two young men.

"This is risky business. What exactly do you need from me?" he finally asked.

"We need a car and place to hold Seidman. We figure you can provide both," Khalil said.

"That I can do," Juno said slowly, still mulling over the proposition. "I can give you a black Lincoln town car and a room in the basement to hold him in. It's the place I bring my chicas when I want some pussy. It's got a bed, a TV, a refrigerator and a bathroom off to the side. Perfect to hold someone for a few days."

"Are you sure you want to do this? You're not going to back out at the last minute?" Doo asked.

Juno paused for a minute before looking over at Khalil and Doo. They were both street-smart niggas who had never let him down. Plus, they knew when to think with their heads and when to use their fists.

"Yeah man. I trust you. I have done business with you for the last two years and have never had problems. But mainly, I am doing this for my family and my people. You know the Garafuna live by the water. We make a living by fishing. But now, the government of Honduras wants to push us out and put up a hotel for rich gringo tourists. With two million dollars I can buy the houses my family lives in and bribe the government officials so that they will build the hotel somewhere else."

"Damn, Juno, that shit is cold," Khalil said

"*Tu sabes*. People call us gangsters because we steal cars and sell the parts on the black market. But the biggest gangsters in the world are the people who own banks and run governments. That's why I have no problem kidnapping this motherfucker! If I can save my family by taking money from his family, that's fine with me. He's probably a bigger thief than we are!"

"You speak the truth, Brother Man," Doo said. "The same thing is happening in the Bronx. Big companies are buying buildings, raising the rent and forcing people and businesses out. The rent on my father's store has been raised twice in the last year. That's why I'm in."

"Let's put our hands together," Khalil said." We're all brothers, and we're in this to the bitter end."

The three men joined hands on Juno's desk and then got up and hugged one another. The plan was ready. Rasheeda would set the day and time of the kidnapping. Juno would give them the town car they needed, and they would bring Seidman back to the garage and negotiate. If the plan worked, their lives would be changed forever. If it didn't, well, it would just mean their bad luck got a whole lot worse.

CHAPTER **26**

Rasheeda didn't end up going to meet the Doc that Friday. In fact, it was the next Wednesday by the time Rasheeda got up the courage to head up to Lehman and face Nelson Temple. Now that she was leaving both Cheetah's and Lehman, life didn't seem real. But Khalil cautioned her to stick to her regular routine, that way they wouldn't draw suspicion later. So while he continued servicing his regular clients and taking his brothers to after-school, Rasheeda spent most of her time at home, taking care of Junior and trying to slow down her mother's drinking. On Saturday she brought Junior over to Erika's to help her study for the GED, but it was hard to lie and not say anything about what they were planning. As she timed Erika's practice test, she thought how this might be the last time she saw her home-girl and felt sick to her stomach.

Later on Monday, Rasheeda was finally able to get her mom out of the house long enough to have some privacy with Khalil.

"Do you really think this is gonna work?" she asked as they lay naked on her bed, staring up at the crumbling plaster of the ceiling.

"Fo' sure, my queen. Fo' sure. Doo and I got it all planned out. All you gotta do is your part."

Rasheeda sighed. "But what are we gonna do after? Where are we gonna go?"

"We'll go wherever the fuck we want, baby. That's the beauty of it. Or we'll stay. You've only missed a few weeks of school. You could catch up. Finish the semester, isn't that what you want?"

"How could we stay? I'd be too nervous to get caught."

"No one's gonna get caught," Khalil said gently. "But then we'll go, wherever you want—so long as you finish school like you always said you was gonna."

"I'll have to start over."

"So what? It's gonna happen for you, for us, baby. I promise."

Rasheeda sighed. "My moms gonna be back any minute. We should get up."

"K," Khalil said pulling on his Sean John jeans and Rocawear hoodie. "You're clear on the plan and everything, though."

"Yeah, got it."

Her thoughts wandering back to the present, Rasheeda could feel her heartbeat quicken as every train stop brought her closer to the campus. Professor Temple was not going to be happy about this, she thought as she rehearsed the story she was going to give him about leaving school. Professor Temple was the first person at Lehman that Rasheeda had really got down with. After all that drama with her business classmates and Temple busting open the boys' kneecap, she had signed up for a course on Black political movements the next semester, not knowing the man who came to defend her and the professor of the class were one and the same. That's where she really got to know the only man she ever trusted besides Khalil. Not only was the class the bomb, but also Rasheeda was able to meet a man whose gaze never wandered to her chest or her behind. Even the guidance counselor, who had told her that her SAT scores were high enough to go to college, let his hand graze her as he led her to the door. But not Doc. Doc told her to go to grad school. Doc told her to think big. Doc told her to finish her education and get out. Doc got her an extension on her tuition after all the shit went down with her moms, and that creepy lawyer who probably charged them too much. The biggest kicker was that Doc was *white*!

Rasheeda chuckled to herself as she remembered walking in to class the first day and coming face to face with a white Black studies professor. She almost walked right out. After all, she had signed up for the class to get away from all the white professors, white students, and Oreos in her business classes. But then he looked her in the eye and nodded at her and that said enough. She flashed back to the huge man with that bat and saw understanding and knowledge about the struggles she had lived, and in his nod, she saw respect for women. Everything flew from there. His big, booming voice reminded her of the preachers she had grown up listening to and his knowledge of the movements seemed so intimate, so passionate. He encouraged her to speak up about where she was from and what she had heard about those times from her elders. For the first time at Lehman, she felt like what she was studying meant something, and what she had to say, was important. She even started to enjoy writing papers and would go over the page limits, melding her personal experience with the historical analysis Doc taught.

Doc even had her over to his house and introduced her to his wifey, a black woman who hugged her and fed her collard greens, with little flecks of chilli pepper in them—so good it reminded Rasheeda of when her grandma used to cooked and brought tears to her eyes. Later, it turned out that Clarice wasn't actually his wife, but his partner of more than twenty years, which didn't strike Rasheeda as strange in any way, seeing as she had never known *any* married couples growing up in the hood. That fact that they were still together after so long was good enough for her. Rocking a different head wrap for every day and big gypsy silver jewelry, she was confident and well spoken. Reflecting on Clarice's style and attitude, Rasheeda thought to herself, this was not a woman who got played by a man. *Especially a white man.* Although the way Doc was—the way he talked and carried himself— she usually forgot he was white.

Rasheeda got off the train and rehearsed her story. Khalil was accepted into a special education program for ex-convicts in California, so they were moving. This was an opportunity for them. She couldn't pay her tuition anyway. She would reapply to some school out there once they got on their feet. Taking a deep breath, Rasheeda stood outside the door looking at the Doc's nameplate. It read, 'Nelson Temple, Director of Urban Studies, Professor of African American Studies'. She wondered how he did it—all that school, all that work. But then she realized she really didn't know a damn thing about Doc, except that he was real with her. She had no idea where he was from or where he grew up. He seemed to know about the ghetto and understood her life, and there were some rumors that he had been in the Weatherman, a radical group close to the Panthers. Some even said he took part in a bombing that killed people, but other than all the whispers around school, she just knew he was someone to count on.

"Rasheeda, is that you breathing outside my door?" the loud, deep voice of Dr. Temple boomed. Rasheeda jumped. She was startled, and did not answer.

"Well standing out there ain't gonna solve your problems, so you might as well come in, sit your ass down, and eat some of this lunch I ordered from Joe's."

Rasheeda smiled, licking her lips. Joe's was her favorite barbecue spot around. She could eat a rack of their ribs all by herself. Pushing the door open, Rasheeda laughed out loud at the sight of Nelson Temple, bib and everything, just covered in barbecue sauce. Papers were piled high covering the entirety of his desk and with books two rows deep, the bookshelves looked like they could tumble over any moment. Definitely, the office was too small for the Doc, Rasheeda thought to herself. But then again, so was all of Lehman. Not only did the Doc have a big, booming voice and intimidating personality, but he was also an imposing figure. Standing at six-feet-four and built like a boxer, Rasheeda remembered Clarice complaining about how they always had to go to a tailor to make him clothes, because everything else was too tight or short or small. His slightly graying hair was trimmed close and was matched by a thick salt-and-pepper moustache.

"Hey Doc, how's it shakin'? I'd shake your hand but it looks like you're occupying both of them," Rasheeda said, grabbing a seat on an old, worn-down red leather couch.

"Grab a fork. I got the yams and mac and cheese you like."

"Thanks Doc, but you don't have to buy me lunch all the time."

"I bought me lunch, you eating some allows me to get more sides. Now, let's cut the crap, R! Is it tuition again?" Dr. Temple stared into Rasheeda's eyes. She always felt like the look went straight to her gut. It wasn't gonna be easy to lie to this man, she thought, lowering her eyes.

"Yeah. I got suspended at work and they won't give me an extension," Rasheeda said, playing with the plastic fork.

"I'll talk to them. You looked at classes for next semester yet? There's a great class on slavery. You should take it—complete the African American studies major. It'll make you a stronger candidate for the MBA."

"There isn't gonna be a next semester," Rasheeda said quietly.

"What? Don't start with me, girl. You can reapply for financial aid, and if you don't get it again, I will loan you the money myself," Dr. Temple said with such conviction that Rasheeda wondered if that was what having a dad was like.

The problem was, he wasn't her dad and she couldn't take his money any more than she could keep stripping or keep living with how people looked at her because they knew she stripped. It wouldn't change even if he could figure out a way for her to stop, to make this whole crazy plan stop.

A way out of the Bronx was in sight now and she couldn't imagine staying a minute longer than she had to. She'd always be that slut ho at Lehman, that girl who slept with Wall Street to move up. They'd probably start saying she was sleeping with Temple next and she could put that on him. She couldn't tell him all that. She needed a fresh start.

"It's not just the tuition."

"So then, what is it? Lay it all out on the table. We'll work it out."

"It's Khalil."

"Uh-huh," Temple said, raising one eyebrow, putting down a rib, and crossing his arms.

"Khalil got into this new rehabilitation program in California. It's gonna help him go to college, get a good job. It's a brand new program, and I'm gonna move with him."

"So you're gonna drop outta college, so Khalil can go to college? It sounds like a great opportunity, but it doesn't make any sense."

"I was gonna withdraw anyways. Once we get settled out there, I'm gonna reapply to a school out there, get my credits transferred." Rasheeda finally met Dr. Temple's gaze, trying to look reassuring and responsible.

Dr. Temple squinted, drumming his fingers on his paper-covered desk. "There's something you're not telling me."

"That's it really. It's for the best, were getting out, together." Rasheeda could feel her voice waver.

"Nope. There's something you're not telling me."

Rasheeda took her fork and stabbed at the mac and cheese, filling her mouth full of creamy, rich cheese.

"I can't always tell you everything."

"You can, but you don't have to." Temple sighed. "I'm just sad to see my favorite student go. I really do hope it's for the best. Nothing against Khalil, but you got to think about yourself first."

"I know. But this way we can both do good." Rasheeda said, taking another bite of mac and cheese. "I love him, Doc."

"Look, just know if it doesn't work out or if you need anything, I'm here. Day or night. You have my cell phone number. I've seen too much to judge anyone or think less of you."

"Thanks, Doc."

"You're welcome. Now take the rest of this food and let me get back to work."

Rasheeda stood up and grabbed the carton. Pausing at the door, Rasheeda turned to take one last look at Doc. His nose was already back buried in his mound of papers.

"Hey, Doc, is it true that you were in that group the Weatherman that blew up a building?"

Not looking up, he said, "When you get your degree, I'll let you know the big secret."

"Cool. Thanks."

As Rasheeda grabbed the door, she heard her name, this time much softer than she had ever heard Temple's voice sound before.

"Yeah?"

"Good luck. And remember, I'm here."

Rasheeda smiled and walked out, momentarily calmed by Nelson Temple's presence. As soon as she stepped out into the street however, she remembered what was up ahead. Tomorrow, she went back to work. Tomorrow would decide her future. Tomorrow, she was either gonna get out or die tryin'.

CHAPTER **27**

That night, as Rasheeda returned home, she was more determined than ever to get her and her family out of the ghetto. Her moms had already spent all the money she left for Junior on booze. He was hungry, and crying in his crib wearing a soiled diaper. He may have been there for hours like that, there was no way to tell. To top it all off, the heat in the building seemed to be off and the apartment was freezing.

"Moms, moms. Get up," Rasheeda said, shaking her mother fiercely. Her mother opened one eye before shutting it again and burying herself further into the couch.

"The baby's cryin'," her mother slurred.

"Well, then get up! It's your baby, not mine," Rasheeda said, shaking her again. "Did you at least buy some more diapers or formula or anything?"

"Momma's tired," she responded, entering back into a booze stupor. Rasheeda sighed. Shaking her was no use. She'd probably been drinking since the moment Rasheeda left around ten that morning. Rasheeda sighed.

After fiddling with the radiator to try and get it to let out a little heat, Rasheeda grabbed her purse and headed back out into the cold. Once at the store, she bought diapers, formula, baby food, rice, black-eyed peas, vegetables and chicken for a stew. Rasheeda hoped if she at least left her mom something decent to eat while she was gone for the next few days, Junior would be okay until the job was done. After hauling everything back, Rasheeda bathed and fed Junior, put him to sleep, cooked chicken stew, ate, coaxed her mom to eat a bit, and cleaned up the apartment. Exhausted, Rasheeda climbed into bed at ten p.m. unable to even think of the new life to come if the plan went well. Hearing Khalil's ring on her phone, Rasheeda quickly sat up and searched around for her phone. She had forgotten that she needed to charge that, too.

"Hey, baby," she said, answering on the third ring.

"Hey, my Queen. I just wanted to see how you holdin' up."

Rasheeda lay back down. "Yeah, just dozin'."

"You okay? It's barely past ten."

"Yeah, but this house was a disaster and I just had to make sure Junior was set up, you know, for the next few days."

"I'm sorry, baby. You wanna ask Erika to check in?"

Rasheeda sighed. "I don't wanna involve anyone else. It'll be okay."

"It's gonna be more than okay, girl. It's gonna be a whole new life, for all of us. With the money we get, we can take care of our families for real."

"Okay." Rasheeda cradled the phone in her arm, missing the warmth of Khalil's body next to hers.

"And you sure it's all set for tomorrow?"

"Yeah, he called me himself asking where I'd been this week. It's a date. Eight p.m."

"Ok, my Queen. Then get some rest. Just imagine everything that's to come."

"Yeah. You right. I love you, baby."

"I love you, too."

Rasheeda hung up the phone, trying to calm her pounding heart. Lying back, she prayed for the health and safety of everyone she loved, but most of all, she prayed for herself and for Khalil.

CHAPTER **28**

Rasheeda woke up the next morning in a sweat. Grabbing her phone, she was shocked to see it read ten a.m. Twelve hours! She had never slept twelve hours in her life! Hearing Junior's gentle cry, she pulled herself out of bed and stumbled into the kitchen to find her mom standing over the stove.

"Mom? Mom? What's going on?"

"Well hello, lazy bones. What do you mean what's goin' on? I'm cooking breakfast."

"B... breakfast?" Rasheeda stuttered. She hadn't seen breakfast in this house since her dad took off all those years ago. "What's gotten into you?"

"Nothin'," she said, handing Rasheeda a plate of scrambled eggs and bean and potato hash. "I just felt like getting up and makin' breakfast. Can't a mother make her daughter breakfast?"

"I guess so," Rasheeda said, stumbling to take a seat on the couch. Then it hit her. Since her father took off, there was only one reason why her moms ever took care of herself or them.

"You met a man."

"Oh, sweetie, let me tell you, this is more than just a man!"

"Uh-huh," Rasheeda said, burying her face in eggs. She hoped at least this one lasted long enough for her moms to take care of Junior over the next couple days.

Finishing up her eggs, Rasheeda handed her plate to her mom and kissed her on the cheek. "Thanks, Mom. It was real good," she said before heading off to the shower.

"Well, don't you want to hear about him?" her voice trailed Rasheeda.

"Later, Mom, later. I gotta get ready for work."

Closing the door to the bathroom, Rasheeda turned to the shower, hoping for hot water. "Honestly, I don't give a rat's ass about whatever man is gonna be the five hundredth one to leave you," Rasheeda mumbled under her breath.

By one p.m., Rasheeda was dressed and ready to go for her last night at Cheetah's. And she was dressed for it too. Today, she wore a peach colored lacy thong and matching bra that showed off her nipples to perfection. She had covered her dark brown skin with a sparkling body lotion that made her every movement shimmer in the light. Finally, she laced a number of long, thin gold chains over her body. She had even stopped by the nail place to get a French manicure. Checking her phone, she made the final trek to the club. There was no way she was gonna be late and pay extra again to work.

The night went by in a daze. Rasheeda made sure to stay under Ray's radar, smiling and flirting with every customer who approached her. She wasn't gonna be called uppity tonight, she thought. She wanted to drink so badly to calm her nerves but she wanted to make sure she was on top of her game.

"*Hola chica*," Rasheeda heard behind her as she waited for her turn on the pole. No mistake, it was definitely Monica's characteristically over-accented Puerto Rican Spanish. "How was your vacay?"

"Ha, vacay. That's a joke. Long and poor. Now I gotta get back to makin' that paper."

"Don't you know it—that was wack what Ray did. No joke. Men can be such dicks sometimes."

"Yeah, but if they weren't, how would we make money off 'em?"

Monica laughed, turning to the mirror to check her makeup. Rasheeda glanced at her watch again. It was 8:15. What if Money Bags didn't show? Everything was riding on this, on her.

"*Oye chica*, you waitin' for someone or something?" Monica said, turning to face Rasheeda.

"No, girl. Just Khalil. He said he might catch up with me later."

"What, a whole week off and you two still haven't had enough of each other?"

"Whateva, girl. Don't be green, the color don't suit you," Rasheeda mocked back, chuckling.

"I'm just sayin', if you don't wanna work, I'd be happy to take Money Bags off your hands."

"Money?" Rasheeda said slowly.

"Girl, calm down. I just wanted to let you know he arrived and was askin' about you."

"So, what you do with him?" Rasheeda asked, licking her lips. She could feel her nerves getting the best of her.

"What probably no other girl in this club would do—I got him his scotch, signed him up for the private hour, and left him waiting by the pole."

Rasheeda turned away, feeling tears in her eyes. She was gonna miss that loudmouth crazy Puerto Rican. She always had her back. And Erika, too. She was good people, just trying to get out, too. Maybe they could leave them some money too or something.

"*Chica, chica, estás bien?"*

Rasheeda smiled hearing a song from Chase Cross. "Yeah, yeah. Just visualizing that paper, makin' things happen. Hey, that's my cue."

Monica made a face. "You playin' that reggae again?"

"Girl, you know reggae lets me show off my assets," Rasheeda said, shaking her booty before preparing to get on stage. "Hey."

"What now?" Monica said, having already returned to her primping.

"Thanks for always having my back."

"Don't go soft, *chica*, us bad-ass chicks gotta stick together."

Leaving Monica in the dressing room, Rasheeda strutted on the platform, letting Chase Cross' dreams of "Better Dayz" wash over her. As she grabbed the pole and slid down, she realized that this would be her last time. Throwing her head back, she rolled over to face Money Bags, who was clutching his scotch tightly by the stage. His eyes enthralled with her every movement. Breaking into a huge grin, Rasheeda crawled forward slowly displaying her ample cleavage to its best. Leaning over the stage, she planted a sensuous kiss on Money Bags before whispering in his ear, "Hey, baby. I missed you. I got a special night planned for us." Money Bag shifted in his seat, gulping back a large drink of scotch.

As soon as the song was over, Rasheeda strutted down the stage and placed herself in Money Bags' lap.

"So, you ready for Cheetah's Full Service Treatment?"

"What exactly does that entail?" Money asked.

"Anything," Rasheeda said seductively, feeling Money's small dick begin to harden on her thigh. "Come on, let's go," she said, not waiting for a response.

When they arrived in the room, Money Bags grabbed Rasheeda and pressed his wrinkled white lips against hers while grabbing her ass. Rasheeda almost wanted to push him away, but she thought of Khalil and all the people that were counting on her. One more time, she thought to herself. Just one more time.

Pushing him away gently, she smiled again. "What's the rush, baby? We got plenty of time."

Money Bags tried to grope at her again. "Come on, Rasheeda," he said, grabbing her breast.

Rasheeda sharply pushed him down onto the couch, trying to hide her anger and resentment with coyness.

"This is the full-service treatment. That means it's all about you, baby. You gonna let me service you, like you deserve?"

Money Bags nodded.

"Good."

Rasheeda went over to the minibar and pulled out a bottle of Veuve Clicquot. She had to use up at least an hour or people at the club would get suspicious about her and Money disappearing. After pouring the champagne, Rasheeda slowly began to dance in front of Money removing chain by chain and finally her top, until she was left only in her light peach thong. Seeing him grow restless, Rasheeda continued dancing, but began to fondle herself, first playing with her nipples, and then working her way down to her pussy. It was almost as if Khalil was there touching her and she was surprised to find herself wet.

"Hmm-m-m, damn. Look at you making me wet."

"Come over here."

"Okay, but until I say so, I get to do all the touching. I just wanna feel your body. Is that okay?"

Money nodded, intoxicated by the sight of a beautiful black woman pleasuring herself and the constant refills Rasheeda was careful to pour. Again, moving slowly, Rasheeda loosened Money's tie, unbuttoned his shirt and removed his undershirt, slowly licking and caressing every part of his body.

He tasted like Bengay. As she worked her way down to his pants, Money began to moan and shake. Damn, Rasheeda thought, he sounds like a teenager, ready to cum at any moment. Not like Khalil. That man knew the pleasure of taking his time. Now only in his briefs, Money forcefully pushed her face toward his package.

"Not so fast, baby. Let me feel you."

Placing his hand on her breast, Rasheeda kissed Money Bags with as much passion as she could muster while snaking her hand down to his package. Placing her hand on his dick, she began to move her hand up and down the already-hard member. It didn't take long—within a matter of minutes, he had cum and was rushing to catch his breath.

"Hmm, baby, let me clean up and get you a drink—we still got a lot of fun to go."

Rasheeda stepped into the private bathroom and washed her hands with soap and water, before grabbing her phone and texting, *one last drink xo* to Khalil. Pulling out the GHB, Rasheeda chuckled to herself. It was nice that for once, a man would be on the receiving end of the date-rape drug.

Rasheeda sat down next to Money Bags naked, except for his briefs, and furiously typing on his Blackberry.

"Here, I got you a new scotch," she said, stroking his balding head.

Barely acknowledging her as he typed away, he took the glass and downed the entire contents in one shot.

"Damn, baby," she said, without a response from Money.

Rasheeda returned to the bathroom and pulled on the Juicy sweat suit she had stashed earlier in the supply closet. Pulling out her phone once more, she texted Monica. *Money's done. Some business meeting. Not feeling well, takin' a cab home. See you later. Xoxo R.* Then, Rasheeda went to the back door, pushing it open to see Khalil and Doo and motioned them closer.

"You ready?" she said.

"Born ready." Khalil said back, giving her a reassuring smile.

"Good, 'cuz tonight was my last dance. I ain't never comin' back here again."

CHAPTER **29**

Khalil and Mamadou sat in the black Lincoln town car by the back alley of Cheetah's, waiting for Rasheeda to text them when it was time to grab their victim. It was an industrial district, so there was no street traffic at ten p.m. So far, the plan was money.

Receiving Rasheeda's text, Khalil tapped Mamadou on the shoulder. They left the car and walked about twenty yards to the back door of Cheetah's. The door was set in a windowless gray brick wall with trashcans lined up on either side. Across the alley was another wall, painted black, about twenty feet high. It was the back of a warehouse that had no activity at night. Khalil was pleased to see that no apartment buildings were visible from where they would be making the grab. The only sound was the music pumping from Cheetah's, and the crunching of broken glass under their feet as they walked through the alley in silence.

Rasheeda, a blue sweater covering her top, but her beautiful legs still bare, opened the door for them. Khalil couldn't believe how beautiful she looked, even in just a simple sweatshirt. It made him even more determined for this to be her last dance.

"This way," she whispered, and pointed them through an open door where a small gray haired man lay sprawled and unconscious on a red cushioned chair—his fly unzipped and stains on his pants. The room was surrounded by mirrors and lit by colored lamps.

"He's out cold."

"Doo, let's make this happen," Khalil said. "You grab him under one shoulder and I'll grab him under the other. We're gonna carry him out upright with his feet dragging along the ground, like he's just another guy at the strip club who got drunk and needs to be taken home."

"Word, Khalil," Mamadou said, nodding. "That way people think we just car service people helping out a customer."

"Rasheeda, you walk out first and make sure that Five-O isn't around. But if they are, just tell them we got a drunk on our hands."

Rasheeda quickly slid her pants on over her G-string and wrapped a coat around her shoulders. She walked into the alley, looked around, and called out, "It's clear."

Doo and Khalil picked up Money Bags and carried him toward the door.

"See, Doo, this shit is easy," Khalil said as they carried him into the alley and shut the door behind them." Just like that movie *Weekend at*

Bernie's, thought Khalil, remembering the film where two young guys spent a vacation weekend in the Hamptons with a corpse, pretending he was alive.

"Yeah, this fool weighs almost nothing," Doo replied. "But is this skinny, small-dick muthafucka really one of the richest men in New York City? He wouldn't last ten minutes in the South Bronx."

"Don't be so sure, Doo," Khalil said, unlocking the car via remote. "The only size that matters when you're getting your hustle on is the size of your brain. The same shit that works on Wall Street would probably work down here. This motherfucker probably be running the crack trade in the neighborhood and have a string of bitches on his skinny dick."

While Rasheeda stood looking for police or passersby, the two men approached the entrance of the alley, carrying Money Bags with little effort. When Rasheeda gave them the signal, they opened the back door of the car and lay Money Bags down on the back seat. Mamadou joined their victim, sitting down by the unconscious man's head. Meanwhile, Khalil slid into the drivers' seat and Rasheeda sat next to him on the passenger side. They slammed the doors shut and looked around. Still no police. Time to roll.

Khalil pulled the car into the street and made a left turn onto Bruckner Boulevard. It was a mile and a half to Juno's garage in Hunts Point, but Khalil didn't worry about being stopped. In the neighborhoods they were driving through, a Lincoln town car meant car service, the primary means of nighttime transportation in a part of the city where yellow cabs never came. They could be people heading to or from work, a party or a drug deal. No one gave them a second glance.

"Yo Rasheeda," Khalil said as they turned onto Hunts Point Avenue. "You have people covering for you at the club?"

"Don't worry about it. We booked the room for the night. They'll just assume I've made Money Bags my private client and am going with him to a hotel. Shit like this happens all the time. The manager doesn't care so long as the client pays the club for what goes on in the private room."

"Damn, girl, that sounds just like prostitution!"

"Stripping ain't the half of it. Regular lap dances are $20—the only real money is getting up front and personal with the customers, which means getting their dick hard and busting their nut. If you can do it without putting their shit in your pussy, cool, but its all about getting them off. If you don't get them off, the money you be seeing won't pay your bills," Rasheeda prattled nervously. She couldn't believe how much she was talkin'—the nerves must really be getting to her. She grabbed Khalil's hand to steady herself.

"They won't be suspicious that Money Bags just disappears out the back door?" Mamadou asked from the back.

"Nah, if he's taking me to a hotel, they damn sure don't want him going out the front door. He's a high roller and wants his privacy respected. That's how they stay in business." Rasheeda leaned over to kiss Khalil, trying to hide her worries. At least that was what she heard—she hopped Candy's stories were true about staying at the W or Marriot with guys she met at Cheetah's.

"Well that just shows we smarter than other niggas," Khalil said. "Or else we just crazy and ready to die."

Still holding Khalil's hand, Rasheeda squeezed gently. "Don't say that, boo."

The car slowly eased out of blocks of stores and apartment buildings into a maze of warehouses and garages. Not a soul was on these streets. They turned left onto the block where Juno's garage stood, which, with its broken streetlights, darkened buildings, and large trucks parked on the curb, looked like the land that God forgot. If Money Bags died tonight, he would certainly not be the first murder victim to disappear into the black hole that was Hunts Point.

Pulling up outside the garage, Khalil sent a text to Juno. Seconds later he heard a large metal door roll up on the building right in front of him. Smoothly, Khalil drove into a warehouse filled with cars and auto parts before the door descended behind them. Juno walked up to the car with a smile on his face. Khalil rolled down his window.

"*Hola, mis amigos*. I see you have your prize," Juno said as he looked into the back of the town car. "Get him out and we'll take him to my hideaway."

As Rasheeda got out of the car, the huge smile on Juno's face grew even bigger.

"Wow, *mami*. Now this is a woman worth dying for!" he said, picking up her hand and kissing it. "Is this your girl from the club?" he said to Khalil before turning back to Rasheeda. "*Bueno, mami*, if you ever get tired of Khalil and want a mature man to take care of you, please look me up. You know lovers, like wine, get better with age," he said with a wink, "

"Thank you, Juno, but I've had enough of mature men to last me a lifetime," Rasheeda said relieved that she would never ever, ever have to step back in Cheetah's again. It had taken everything she had just to go back that night for a few hours and let Seidman slobber all over her. Rasheeda turned to the passed out body in disgust.

"Look at this clown we just brought here. He thinks he is God's gift to women and he can't last but two minutes by the time he gets hard. Plus, he slobbers when he kisses me. It's disgusting. If this is mature, give me young every time."

Juno laughed. "Well, *mi princesa*, I had to try. When a Latin man stops trying to make love to every woman he sees, he is ready for the grave."

"Hey, Juno, stop thinking about your dick and leave my boo alone," Khalil said with a smile. "We need to take Seidman to the place we're going to keep him."

While Mamadou and Khalil picked up their captive by the shoulders, Juno led them through rows of cars to a door in the back of the garage. He opened it and revealed a staircase, painted the same gray color as the walls surrounding it. Following Juno through an open door, they entered a room that looked like MTV Cribs had decorated it. A king-sized bed with red covers sat in one corner, a flat-screen TV hung on the opposite wall, and a plush purple lounge chair sat next to a bar of steel and mirrors filled with liquors of every imaginable variety. A door next to the bar led to a spotlessly clean bathroom with new fixtures.

"Damn, Juno, this is sweet," Mamadou called out. "How many chicas have you brought down here?"

"More than you can count, *mijo,* more than you can count."

"Where do you want to put him?" Khalil asked.

"Let's put him on the bed while he's still out and tie his hand in front of him," Doo said. "Then we'll tie him to the chair and have him wake up in that position."

Hoisting Money onto the bed, Doo continued, "Juno, do you have any food in the fridge? We want to make sure he gets plenty to eat and drink. This whole thing will work best if he feels we are going to treat him well."

"I have enough food to last for three days. This man is going to eat better than he does at home. By the time this man leaves, he will love us."

"Damn, my professor talked about that once," Rasheeda said, "He called it the 'Stockholm Syndrome'."

"I don't know what it's called," Doo said, "but the best way to break people is go back and forth between torturing them and making them feel comfortable. That's what they used to do in my country to people who opposed the government. Most of them broke and gave up their friends."

Khalil and Doo looked at their captive, now collapsed on the soft comforter. Khalil took some twine he had in his pocket and wrapped it expertly around Seidman's wrists.

"Now, lets move him to the chair," Khalil said as he tied the last knot. "Hold his shoulders, Doo." Khalil coiled the rope in a circle that pinned Seidman's waist to the back of the chair, while Doo held him in place. After six revolutions of the rope, and several knots, Seidman, still out cold, had been secured in an upright position. His feet were on the ground and his hands tied in front of him.

"He'll wake up soon," Khalil said pulling out his .38. "So he needs to see your machete. Even if we don't shoot him, I'd like him to think about one of his body parts being chopped off if he doesn't cooperate."

The four conspirators walked over to the bar and sat on the stools in front of it, facing Seidman. Juno took out a bottle of Courvoisier and poured them each a glass. They raised their glasses in a toast as Khalil called out "To better days for all of us." They clicked glasses in triumph, in hope and in fear. Now the waiting began.

CHAPTER **30**

A half and an hour later, at 11:30 PM, Seidman slowly awoke. First his eyes opened and darted around taking in his new setting. Then he spoke, "Where the fuck am I? Who the fuck are you?" His eyes scanning the room in a confused daze.

"Rasheeda? Is that you?" he said. The kidnappers were still enjoying a few drinks at Juno's bar, so when no one answered Seidman, he began to struggle in the chair.

"Rasheeda!" He shouted. "I can't believe you are mixed up with these thugs. How could you do this to me after all I've done for you? I thought we had something special."

Putting down her Courvoisier, Rasheeda walked over to face him.

"Special? Who are you kidding? We had a business relationship. You gave me money and I gave you fantasy sex. I was nothing to you but a Black body to use as a plaything."

"I loved my time with you. It was the best part of my week."

"You had a funny way of showing it—like that time you made fun of me to entertain your Wall Street friends." Rasheeda crossed her arms. "Did your ever ask about my life outside the strip club? Did you ever try to talk to me about anything important? Did you ever try to teach me something about your business? You don't know the first thing about who I am. Maybe if you showed the slightest interest in *me*, I wouldn't have started to hate your saggy white ass. As far as I'm concerned, you're getting exactly what you deserve."

Turning away, Rasheeda walked back over to the group and put her arms around Khalil. Seidman struggled with the rope to little avail.

"Well what you deserve, you ungrateful bitch is life in prison, which is exactly what you and your stupid thug partners are going to get." As Seidman ranted Rasheeda grabbed Khalil tightly.

"Do you know who I am? Do you know who my friends are? Politicians, lawyers, judges. When this is over—even if you don't totally fuck it up—my people are going to chase you to the ends of the earth."

"Motherfucker, you don't get it." Khalil said, approaching Seidman, "You're acting like you still run things. Down here, you ain't shit. You my bitch. You do what I say, or you get hurt."

"You're playing out of your league," Seidman said, his face contorting in anger and contempt. "Why don't you all just let me go and go back to your pathetic lives? I'll give you ten thousand dollars and we'll call it even."

"I like the ten, but the other part is off. We want ten million!" Khalil said bringing his face within an inch of Seidman's.

"Where do you think you are going to find ten millions dollars?" Seidman said struggling with his ropes again.

Khalil backed off, pausing for emphasis. "Well, in a few minutes we're going to call your wife and tell her that if she doesn't come up with the money, we're going to kill you and make your grandchildren disappear."

"You leave my grandchildren out of it or I'll hire people to kill you all when this is over," Seidman said quietly but deliberately.

Khalil looked over at Mamadou and Juno who were still calmly sipping at their drinks. The three began to laugh.

"There are only two ways this is going to be over: when you die or we get the money," Khalil said. "Doo, call this motherfucker's wife."

"You're all fools. You don't know what you're getting yourself into," Seidman said, a worried look suddenly coming across his face. "It's not what you think. You'll see. This is going to turn out very badly."

While Mamadou left the room and went upstairs to Juno's office, Khalil, Juno and Rasheeda sat ignoring the threats of their captive and watched BET. They trusted Mamadou, who had learned the workings of Wall Street in his business courses, and who seemed to have no fear, in handling the communications with Seidman's wife.

Upstairs, Mamadou pulled out the throwaway cell he had purchased for the occasion, and dialed the number of Seidman's home. When Seidman's wife picked up, he calmly and coldly told her Seidman and been kidnapped and gave her precise instructions as to what she had to do to save his life and protect her family. As expected, the mention of the grandchildren sent her into a panic. She promised to go to the bank vault and take out ten million dollars worth of certificates in Seidman's stock, and redeem them into cash. When she had the money, she was going to call Mamadou to arrange a drop.

Mamadou returned to the room where Seidman was being held and told everyone what was going on. Khalil and Rasheeda hugged one another, but a strange look came over Seidman's face.

Now, the real waiting began. Khalil untied Seidman, and with Juno's help, led him to the bathroom to relieve himself while Rasheeda took sandwiches out of the refrigerator. When he returned, Khalil retied Seidman to the chair, while Juno untied his hands. Soon, the four kidnappers were eating sandwiches with their captive, and downing glasses of wine and beer. Now that Seidman had decided to be silent, the atmosphere was almost calm.

After eating, Rasheeda and Khalil went to the bed to take a nap while Juno trained Khalil's gun on Seidman. After sleeping a few hours, Rasheeda and Khalil took the gun from Juno and guarded Seidman while he and Mamadou lay down to rest. It was now five a.m. on Friday morning.

"Khalil, what will we do when we get the money?" Rasheeda whispered. "How will we keep them from comin' after us?"

Khalil stroked Rasheeda's back and spoke to her in a low, gentle voice. "These people have so much money that ten million dollars is like ten dollars to us. So long as we don't hurt Seidman, they won't say a word. They don't want it getting out that he was going to a strip club in the Bronx twice a week for the last year."

As Rasheeda lay her head on his shoulder, Khalil continued. "You saw what happened to Elliot Spitzer when he went to a hooker five or six times? People find out Money Bags was getting lap dances every week and they're not going to want to trust their money with him or want him helping their favorite charities."

Rasheeda snuggled closer. "Khalil, you're so smart. I hope we can get to a place where you don't have to sell drugs and can use your mind to help people."

"Someday, boo. Someday."

CHAPTER **31**

Now well into Friday, the waiting continued for another half a day. Juno went back upstairs to deal with garage business while the three young people waited with their captive. Conversation halted. Seidman actually slept for three or four hours while his captors played cards and watched television. It was just like a scene from the movies and TV shows about kidnappings they had seen growing up.

As Khalil waited, the chorus of a Cormega song ran through his mind. When this was over, would he finally be free of the violence and pain that had always surrounded him, or would he always be a prisoner of the ghetto he grew up in?

Look at my life

you see white coke and black roses

And tears shed for passed soldiers

We all walkin' a path chosen

From the cradle 'til the casket's lowered

I still got the black ski mask to throw on

But I can get richer off the tracks I flow on

I'd be lyin' if I said I wasn't hustlin' no more

With Seidman asleep, and Khalil and Rasheeda lost in their private thoughts, Mamadou's cell phone started buzzing. They all stood up expectantly. This was the call they had been waiting for. Mamadou went to pick up the cell.

"Yeah, this is him. Did you get the securities? … Do you have the money?" Rasheeda grabbed Khalil's hand and squeezed tightly.

Two minutes of silence ensued, then Mamadou's voice rose higher.

"What do you mean the securities are worthless? What do you mean there is no money?"

Silence again.

"You're broke? … The government seized the accounts? The whole thing was a fraud? Then where's the money?" Mamadou turned his back to the others, but his aggravated voice rang loud and clear.

More silence. Rasheeda squeezed Khalil's hand tighter in a panic.

"What do you mean you didn't know your husband was running a scam?" Mamadou yelled into the phone. "He tricked you just like he tricked his clients?"

"Well, what are you going to do to get him released?" Mamadou's lowered his voice now, speaking slowly and deliberately. "You still have your apartment and four houses? Can't you sell one of them to get the ransom? Yes, I know it's a depression but sell a house, sell a kidney. I don't give a damn. Get us the money if you want to see your husband alive again."

More silence.

"What did you say? That's cold. You mean you really don't care if he dies? You actually want us to kill him? Well, if that's how you feel, I guess we're all fucked!" Doo hung up the cell phone and threw it to the ground. By now, Mamadou had turned back to face the others. He was looking straight at Khalil in a fit of pure rage. "It looks like people in the South Bronx aren't the only ones getting fucked by the people on Wall Street," he said.

Not sure what to do, Khalil and Rasheeda watched as he walked over to Seidman and slapped him hard across the face, five times, waking him up instantly and drawing a trickle of blood from his mouth. Rasheeda and Khalil stood still, not fully understanding the situation.

"You motherfucker! You pig! You cum-sucking, ass-licking dog! You not only hustled us, you hustled your wife and everyone who invested with you," Doo said, slapping Seidman again before punching him in the stomach. "Your investment trust is worthless because half the investments you said you made never existed and the other half are in companies that tanked! Where'd the money go, nigga? Where did it go?"

"Stop! Stop! If you stop hitting me, I'll tell you," Seidman managed to say. "You didn't listen when I told you this whole thing was going to end badly! You should have taken the ten grand and let me go."

Doo backed off, threateningly pulling his machete while Rasheeda clung desperately to Khalil, her heart beating quickly.

"My whole business was what they call a Ponzi scheme. People put their money in thinking I was going to invest it, but I spent most of the money and kept just enough around to pay them their interest. Since most people saw their money growing they never tried to redeem the full value of their securities and if they did, there were enough new people putting their money in to pay them the full amount. It all worked perfectly until a year ago when the recession hit and lots of people started needing money to pay their bills after they lost their jobs or houses. Now all of a sudden, lots of people started asking for their principal and there wasn't enough there to pay them. Enough people complained to the government and two months ago, the IRS and the SEC started snooping around. When you grabbed me, I still hadn't heard anything about the results of the investigation, but it looks like they seized everything. I'm fucked, you're fucked, and my wife is fucked. There's no money. You want my house in Aspen—you can have it, but there's no money."

Khalil, Mamadou and Rasheeda watched Seidman's performance in silence, their rage brewing. They had been blindsided and they had been tricked. As much as they believed Seidman's story, they sensed that he was hustling them just like he had hustled his wife and his investors.

Seidman, sensing their confusion, began pleading for his life in honeyed tones that any street criminal would use were they taken prisoner by a rival crew.

"Listen, I know you hate me, but the only way you're going to come out of this in one piece is if I'm alive. If you kill me, the cops are going to track you down, no matter what I did, but if you let me go, I'm going to leave the country and no one will know what happened. I can't go back to my family. I can't go back to my business. If you free me, all the attention will be focused on my fraud. No one will know or care that I was kidnapped before

I left the country. You will be completely safe. You can all go back to doing what you were doing with no harm done."

Khalil listened to Seidman's rap with a growing rage. Walking over to Doo and Seidman, he pulled out his .38 and put it against Seidman's forehead.

"I don't trust a thing this nigga says. He hustled some of the richest and smartest people in New York, so you know he's hustling us. Let's just kill him and put his body in the Bronx River. I'm tired of his motherfucking games. I'm a count to ten and pull the trigger."

"Wait, Khalil," Rasheeda cried out. "Let's think this through before we go off and kill someone. We don't know enough about his finances to tell whether he's lying or not. We need someone who knows this stuff to help us figure out what to do."

"I thought we did know this stuff!" Khalil yelled in anger. "You and Doo, I thought you studied business."

"Baby, I'm only in my third semester, and Doo just finished his associates. We need someone who's been around for longer than that."

"And who do you have in mind with that kind of inside information?" Khalil said not lowering his voice. Rasheeda put her hands on her lips, staring Khalil down.

"Professor Temple. He lectures about this stuff all the time. Remember when he told us that the bailout was just a big hustle to keep Morgan Stanley and Goldman Sachs afloat. Now the papers are all saying the same thing. He knows more about this than anyone."

"Yeah, Rasheeda, maybe he knows this stuff better than we do, but can we trust him?"

Rasheeda thought back to all her lunches, invites to Temple's house and when he fought to get her loans extended. But mostly she thought back to when he came raging down the hall with a bat. If it weren't for Rosa he probably would've killed one of those boys then and there. He may be a professor but he could say some pretty radical things sometimes, things that even shocked her and she heard it all. Meeting Khalil straight in the eyes she replied, "Yes."

"When all is said and done, we may still have to kill Seidman after we find out his real financial information. Will Temple be down with that?"

"I wouldn't worry about that, Khalil," Rasheeda said, a small grin forming on her face. "From what I've heard, Professor Temple has killed a lot more people than you have."

CHAPTER **32**

Rasheeda watched Khalil ponder the options. The truth was Khalil had hurt a lot of people, but as far as Rasheeda knew, he hadn't actually wasted anyone. And if she had anything to do with it, it was gonna stay that way. Mamadou was Khalil's boy, Rasheeda accepted that, but he was also different than Khalil—harder, sharper—in a way that scared her. She couldn't explain it, but she imagined the difference was more than just murder, it was experiencing cold-blooded calculated killing. Rasheeda would do anything to keep her baby's blood from turning to ice. She just hoped Professor Temple was as crazy as they all said he was.

Khalil took a slow breath. "You sure you can trust this dude?"

Rasheeda looked deep into Khalil's eyes. "No doubt."

Khalil looked over to Mamadou and Juno, who both nodded. "You got one day. Otherwise, we blastin' this motherfucker away."

Seidman, still bleeding in the corner, stayed silent.

Rasheeda called a car service and headed straight to Professor Temple's office. By now it was ten a.m. and she was beat from the night at the club and the little bits of sleep she'd gotten. Rubbing her sweating palms on her jump suit, she wondered what the Doc was gonna say. She wasn't worried about him turning her in, but she didn't think she was gonna get a pat on the back either. One thing about Nelson Temple was he told you what he thought and he didn't hold back either, not even to spare anyone's feelings.

Rasheeda thought back to class with Temple, remembering how the basketball team thought African American studies classes would be an easy A and how he intimidated half of them into dropping after just one session. Plus, at least five more gangsta posers had to withdraw after they arrived late more than once to class. With Nelson, you were only allowed to miss one class, and if you were five minutes late, you might as well miss that class because that crazy white man would slam the door in your face if you dared to show up at all. Rasheeda, who always made sure to come fifteen minutes early, loved watching the wannabe badass playas get the door slammed in their faces. She knew right then by Doc's stare downs and door slams that none of them would have lasted a night in her hood that is, except for Nelson Temple.

Rasheeda threw a wad of bills at the cabbie and ran off to Professor Temple's office. She wanted to make sure she got there in time—Fridays was the department meeting. It must have dropped at least fifteen degrees since they'd holed up at Juno's, but Rasheeda barely noticed as she threw her hoodie up and jogged into the building.

When she stepped off the elevator on the eighth floor, she could already hear Temple's booming voice from down the hall.

"Yes, ma'am, that is what I said. No, ma'am, you understood me correctly. I don't care if your son is the starting point guard—if he's gonna crowd in the back of the class, arms crossed, notebook closed and not bother to do the reading, then hell yes, he's gonna be seeing the door to my class... Complain? Sure, complain to the chair of the department—me."

Rasheeda sighed. The semester, school, life, was going on without her. If Temple couldn't help them, this time next week she'd be back in the strip club ... or worse ... jail.

Rasheeda heard the phone slam and turned the corner with a quick, shaky breath. It was now or never she thought to herself.

"Rasheeda!" Nelson Temple said, standing to greet her. "It's so good to see you in these parts."

"Uh-huh, I can see you up to the usual." she said from the office doorway.

"Just keepin' it real. Keepin' it real."

"The players?"

"I think it's gotten worse this year. I mean, what's the point of having my rep if I still gotta deal with these crazy kids? I'm going to have to tell my secretary to put out some new rumors about me."

Rasheeda laughed, remembering when her biggest problem was tuition payments and not getting Temple's door slammed in her face. Thinking about the current situation, she turned away, trying to hide the tears that were struggling to burst free.

"R, what's up?" Temple said, noticing her change of mood. Rasheeda turned back to face him—Doc had never called her R before.

Rasheeda stepped quickly into the office and closed the door behind her.

"I'm in a jam," She said, not meeting Temple's gaze.

"What kind of a jam?"

Still avoiding eye contact, Rasheeda ran her now-sweaty palms over her jumpsuit.

"I can't talk about it here. But it's the shit-don't-blow-over, twenty-to-life type of jam."

Temple crossed the room and placed his large hands on Rasheeda's shoulders.

"Did Khalil get you into something?"

Rasheeda shook her head.

"I got me into something," she said, looking dead into Temple's eyes. "Yeah, Khalil's a part of it, but it was 'cuz of me. He wanted to save me, take care of me. I got me into something by never accepting the ghetto I grew up in."

Temple patted Rasheeda's shoulders before putting his hands in his pockets and pacing over to the window.

"Rosa!" he bellowed.

"What?" Rosa said, appearing in the doorway. Rosa had been with Temple almost a decade now—the only secretary who could put up with his standards and demands. Rasheeda liked Rosa because she grew up in the next building over and always kept it fly, from head to toe. Like today, she was rocking skin-tight jeans, knee-high boots and a skin tight V-neck from DKNY. But she also knew how to take care of businesses; her kids may not have a daddy but they were in every single program or sports team Rosa could get her hands on. Temple liked her because she didn't take any shit and when his ideas were bad, she told him so. Straight up.

Seeing Rasheeda, Rosa wrapped her arms around her. "You okay? Sweetie?"

"She'll be fine," Temple interjected, still facing the window.

"Rosa, cancel all my meetings for the rest of the day."

"Your class?" she asked raising her eyebrows.

"Cancel it," Temple repeated.

"You've never canceled a class."

Temple shrugged. "You're right. Get Greene to teach it." He knew that would tick off the grad student.

Grabbing his coat Temple said, "Let's go."

"Where?" Rasheeda asked, leaving Rosa and following him out of his office and down the hallway.

"I'm hungry," Temple said as he tapped his foot impatiently for the elevator.

"Rosa!" he cried out again.

"Yeah, boss," she said popping her head out of Temple's office.

"And get some better rumors circulating out there about me. People don't remember who the Weathermen or the Black Panthers are anymore." Temple turned his attention back to the door. "Like arson or murder or something? What happened to those ones?"

Before Rosa could answer, Temple swiftly stepped into the elevator almost leaving Rasheeda in the hallway.

CHAPTER **33**

Rasheeda and Temple walked in silence to the car, just the sound of snow crackling under their feet. Lehman's campus looked beautiful in its white cover. Lehman really was the jewel of CUNY, even if it was in the Bronx, Rasheeda thought to herself. She would miss it, even as hard as it had been.

As they drove down Jerome Ave then down the concourse to 149th Street, both Rasheeda and Temple were lost in thought—Rasheeda hoping that Khalil could just hold on, hoping that Temple would know what to do, and Temple reminiscing about the once-vibrant South Bronx and the horrible things he had seen in the '60s and '70s and of course the '80s—the crack '80s that kids like Khalil and Rasheeda were still struggling to overcome more than two decades later.

At 149th Street, Temple turned into Venice Restaurant and Pizzeria. At eleven a.m., it was still early enough to beat most of the lunch crowd but Temple still handed the waiter a couple twenties for some privacy in the back. Plus, as a well-known mob spot, everyone in there, even the local business owners and secretaries who just came in for quality Italian food, knew to mind themselves. As soon as the waiter came, Temple ordered garlic cheese bread, plates of antipasti and pasta and a bottle of red wine.

"Okay," Temple said, taking a large gulp of merlot. "Hit me."

Rasheeda took a big gulp herself before telling her story. "It all started about two weeks ago. I was having trouble payin' my tuition again and then I got suspended from the strip club for refusing to dance for a customer. I know it was stupid but I was just tired and ready to go home. That next night, I was out with Khalil and I broke down. I just didn't—I mean don't wanna strip anymore. I can't take it, especially the Wall Street types that come in. It gives me the hives to let them touch me. But in my situation, there's no way else to make enough money to pay for school."

"You should've come to me," Temple said quietly, although he could feel the rage in him building. Despite decades of community organizing, bright young men and women were still being faced with the same shit.

"Well I didn't," Rasheeda said indignantly. "I went to my boyfriend and that's when all this craziness happened."

"What happened?"

Rasheeda looked around and then leaned in. Quickly, she said, "We kidnapped my richest client. You know Robert Seidman?" When Temple nodded, she continued. "We got him holed up in Hunts Point."

Temple took another big gulp of merlot. "No shit."

Rasheeda nodded. "But the problem is when we called his wife for a ransom we found out he had *no* money! That he been scheming everyone this entire time. I don't know—he called it a Ponzi something? So now, she don't give a fuck what we do with him. We were supposed to get millions—it was our ticket out. Khalil says we're gonna have to kill him."

Rasheeda looked at Temple in desperation. "Sometimes I think I'd rather go to jail than go back to my life before this all. At least it'd be something different."

Quiet for once, Temple leaned back, swirling his glass of wine.

"You don't want to go to jail, Rasheeda. Trust me."

Rasheeda shrugged. "What choice do I have? Hood rats like me got three choices – jail, death, or welfare. It's all the same."

"Not for you," Temple said, sipping. "Now eat up. We got some businesses to take care of."

"You mean you'll help?"

"Rasheeda, you're probably the best student I've ever came across. You think all you got is a brain for numbers, but the papers you wrote for my class last semester were the best I've ever read in all my years of teaching. I'm not letting that go to waste."

Looking away, Rasheeda felt her eyes glisten before turning back and eating her fill of pasta and wine with the only white man she ever imagined trusting.

Back in the car by noon, Rasheeda turned to the imposing man next to her. She couldn't believe that her life, her baby's life was in the hands of a white man. After all these years surrounded by pimps, playas and hustlers, white and black—all her hopes lay in a radical professor. Even with her full stomach, Rasheeda felt the butterflies in her stomach flapping like a ten-pound flounder.

"Damn, the food was da bomb, but … what's the plan?" Rasheeda asked timidly.

"We just have to make a little stop at a friend's and then we can head over to the spot."

Rasheeda nodded, noting their downtown direction. Pretty soon, they were in Harlem, right across from the Douglass Projects where Rasheeda was born. *How these project niggas gonna help me?* Rasheeda thought as she watched Temple get out of the car. Temple walked straight to an old rundown brownstone directly across from the public housing. After being buzzed through, they walked up to the fourth floor and waited.

"Nelson Temple!" Rasheeda heard as the door swung open to reveal a slight African American man with thick black glasses. Temple dwarfed the man by at least six inches but the two embraced warmly anyway.

"This is one of my students, Rasheeda," Temple said, motioning to Rasheeda.

"Lovely to meet you, dear. You sure you don't wanna change professors?" the man said, chuckling as he ushered them into his small but tidy one-bedroom apartment.

"Rasheeda, this is Nathan Powell, an old, old friend," Temple said, looking around at the lack of furnishings. "I guess your money's still going to the same place, since I know for a fact Columbia pays you better than this. Even with the gentrification that's going on in the hood."

"Power to the people!" Nathan Powell chuckled, raising his fists.

Temple turned to Rasheeda, motioning for her to sit down on an old green couch. "I know it doesn't seem like it, but Dr. Powell here is one of

Columbia University's most distinguished chemistry professors."

"Word?" Rasheeda said, looking around at the dilapidated, largely empty apartment.

Her eyes landed on Powell. He was barely taller than she was, and couldn't weigh more than one hundred forty pounds. His graying hair was a nappy mess, and he wore khaki pants with a red Black Power t-shirt. He couldn't have been more different from Temple, Rasheeda thought. Then she said, "I thought the point of going to school was to get out of the ghetto."

Powell winked at Temple. "Good thing I'm from the 'burbs then."

"Huh?"

"I grew up in the suburbs. I know it's hard to believe, but there are still some Black people outside the inner city."

"So then, how'd you end up here?"

"I came to Columbia. Although most of the white professors and students like to ignore it, being at Columbia is being in the ghetto!"

Rasheeda nodded, finding a new respect for a type of black man she had never met before—the educated social activist. Who knew they still existed? As Powell and Temple reminisced, Rasheeda learned how Powell first got involved in the Civil Rights Movement. He accidentally got caught up in a building takeover where he was working in a lab; being black, he got arrested and beat up by an all-white police force anyway. Apparently, Temple and Powell met up in the pen, where Temple made sure no further abuse happened to him. He laid out a couple of hoodlums who thought Powell was an easy mark.

Temple stood up. "Sorry to be abrupt but I need to talk to you for a moment in private," he said motioning to the bedroom.

"Of course," Powell said, becoming serious. The two men headed into the back room and shut the door. After fifteen minutes Temple emerged, smiling, but not in a happy way. It was more of the self-satisfied smile of a man who knew he was going to be getting his revenge.

Quickly, the pair said their goodbyes and headed down the stairs, Rasheeda almost having to jog to keep up with Temple's long strides. His face was a mask of determination, as he drove with purpose. With Rasheeda's directions they were back at Juno's in twenty minutes.

Standing in front of Juno's garage, Temple turned to Rasheeda. "You trust me?"

Rasheeda nodded.

"Good, because I'm gonna help you, but it's not going to be pretty. You down with that?"

"Do I have any other choice?"

"No."

CHAPTER **34**

Back inside Juno's warehouse, Rasheeda ran to Khalil and embraced him tightly. Keeping Khalil's arms around her waist, she turned to face everyone.

"Hey y'all, this is Temple."

Mamadou and Juno didn't move. Arms crossed and expressionless, their eyes scanned over the figure of a six-foot-four older white man bursting at the seams of his suit. He looked like a cross between Hulk Hogan and a construction worker, not like a professor who would know the inner workings of Wall Street. Khalil nodded to the pair and they snapped into action.

"What's good?" said Mamadou.

"*Que pasa?*" said Juno.

"What's the plan?" added Khalil, getting straight to the point.

Temple walked over to the bed, took off his coat and suit jacket and laid them down. Next, he began to unbutton his cuffs and rolled them up to his elbows.

"You just leave this muthafucka to me," Temple growled. "You're in for a treat."

Temple grabbed a chair and dragged it directly in front of Seidman. Sitting down less than a foot away, Temple gave him a menacing smile. Temple didn't lose eye contact for a moment. He had stared down many a man and wasn't about to let a Wall Street crook get the better of him.

"So, I hear that you've been running a little scheme on all your investors. That's pretty street. I respect a man that can hustle."

Seidman blinked nervously. "Yeah, b-but it's all gone now," he stammered. "The cash, the feds. There's nothing left."

Without losing eye contact and without moving from his chair, Temple hit Seidman square in the cheek with a forceful right hook, followed by a swift upper cut. Seidman doubled over in pain.

Temple grabbed his ear and pulled him close. "You may think you can play these kids 'cuz you some big Wall Street type, but you can't fool me. Every hustler has a stash, and a hustler of your stature, damn he's got to have the stash of all stashes."

Temple pushed him back and let his words settle in. He unbuttoned the top three buttons of his shirt, revealing a white wife beater. Abruptly, he got up and walked over to his coat and took out a small plastic container of clear liquid. Strolling back, he winked at Khalil and Mamadou who were now in rapt attention. Juno had excused himself to deal with customers.

"You see this?"

Seidman nodded slowly.

"Good. A friend of mine cooked up this little concoction this afternoon for me. Now, I didn't want to have to use it on you, but I will if I have to. See, in here is an extra potent version of burning acid. You know that stuff that's incredibly painful and will give you fourth-degree burns?"

Seidman nodded again.

"This is not that. *This* won't give you any burn whatsoever—unless you count completely losing whatever touches it." Temple laughed.

Seidman swallowed. "You're lying."

Temple laughed again. "Wanna test me?"

"You're lying. It's probably just soda water."

"You're right. It probably is. So let's check it out, shall we?"

Temple motioned for Khalil and Mamadou to come over. "Hold him down, hard. Don't let him move an inch."

Slowly, Temple removed the cap. "You sure you want to do this, you greedy bastard? All you got to do is part with the money you stole, muthafucka."

Seidman trembled. "There's no money!"

Forcefully, Temple grabbed his right index finger and jammed it into the liquid. Within seconds Seidman's entire finger dissolved, leaving just a stub for a finger. But with the exception of Temple, no one was focused on the finger. Seidman was howling in pain like they had never heard before. Swiftly, Temple put the cap on and sat back, but Mamadou and Khalil stood there in shock as Seidman continued to scream at the top of his lungs. Rasheeda ran to the bathroom and threw up her lunch. She had seen people shot, knew about rape, pimps, playas and hustlers, but she had never heard pure pain like that.

After splashing some water on her face, Rasheeda came out of the bathroom to find Seidman whimpering in his chair, his face covered with tears and Juno back in the room.

"What was that? Man, it sounded like you slowly chopped his dick off or something. I had to clear everyone out downstairs!"

"That might be next," Temple said, nonchalantly.

Even Mamadou looked on with a whole new respect.

"R, you okay?" Temple said.

Rasheeda nodded.

"Good, because I may need your help," Temple said soothingly. "It's almost over."

After everyone settled down a bit, Temple returned to his seat in front of Seidman.

"All right, all right, so we dissolved your finger. We can dissolve the rest and your toes, too, but why draw it out? Just tell me where the money is."

Seidman stared back angrily. "Fuck you," he said clutching his deformed hand. "Dissolve them. There's no money."

Temple sat back in his chair. He was a little impressed with Seidman. Most Wall Street suits would have folded just at the talk of flesh-burning acid. But here he was holding out, like a gangsta. That only meant one thing—there was even more money hidden away that he originally thought—at least a hundred mil.

"R, come over here."

Rasheeda walked over slowly. After what she had just seen, she had no idea what could happen now. "Take his dick out."

Rasheeda looked down, surprised. "You want me to… "

Temple refused to lose eye contact with Seidman. "The man's right, we can burn off every single one of his fingers and toes, but I had something better in mind, so you heard me, take his dick out."

Mamadou and Juno catching on chuckled. This white man was more than gangsta! He was a super thug.

Rasheeda bent over, unbutton his pants and exposed Seidman's small, shriveled dick.

"That's it?" Temple said, to the laughs of Mamadou, Juno, and Khalil. Nodding to Mamadou and Khalil, the two walked over, ready to hold down Seidman again.

Temple picked up the jar of acid and waved it in front of Seidman.

"You're crazy," Seidman said slowly. "Look, there's really no money. I'll sell some stuff, I'll get you some money."

Temple moved the acid between Seidman's legs. "It looks like your playa days are done, even with Viagra. Where's the money?"

"There's no—"

Grabbing Seidman's dick, Temple pulled it toward the acid. "Where's the *goddamn money?*" he bellowed, filling the room with his deep voice.

"*Wait! Stop!* I'll tell you!"

In one swift movement, Temple chucked Seidman's dick to the side, closed the jar, stood up and walked over to the bathroom.

"R, get him to write down the account numbers and the bank, plus any passwords or codes I may need."

Rasheeda nodded. Ten minutes later, Temple emerged, all his buttons redone. He grabbed his jacket, took the paper from Rasheeda and strolled to the door.

"I'm gonna go check these out; make sure Seidman here gets to keep his dick.

Then, I'll transfer the money to a private account and figure out what to do next. I'll be back once the money clears."

Then Temple turned to Seidman who was still shaking in his chair. "Don't go anywhere!"

Rasheeda ran over and gave Temple a hug. "Thank you."

Temple laughed. "No, thank you. This was fun. Brought me back to the old days."

Temple shook hands with Khalil, Juno, and Mamadou. "Be careful, it's almost over, but you can't be sloppy now."

Once Temple left, Rasheeda jumped up and down as Juno and Mamadou exchanged bumps.

"Oh my God! Oh my God! Oh my God!! We gonna get paid!"

"Hell, yeah," Khalil said picking Rasheeda up and twirling her around. "Things are finally looking up for the niggas in the hood."

CHAPTER **35**

A day later, around noon, Temple drove back to the garage, exhausted, but extremely pleased. Not only had he transferred all of Seidman's money to new accounts, but he had set up foolproof systems that allowed the four kidnappers to access the money without attracting suspicion, and for Khalil and Rasheeda to start new lives outside the country.

If everything worked out, this would be the greatest single achievement of the secret revolutionary network, the Peoples' Justice Cadre that Temple had created thirty years ago when the dreams of the '60s had collapsed and America turned to the Right. Composed of '60s radicals who were enraged that America had turned its back on poor people and black people, the PJC had, over the years, done targeted kidnappings of developers and corrupt politicians to get money for schools and community centers, and had helped people in trouble start new identities in and out of the country, but this was going to be the biggest operation they had ever done, and he wanted to make sure everyone knew what was expected of them.

Temple parked his black CRV, filled with papers, discarded coffee cups and crumbs of a hundred snacks near the garage and walked through the entrance and headed to the basement. Mostly, he thought about what came next.

Rasheeda was one of the smartest students he had ever worked with, and Mamadou and Juno, as immigrants from the Global South, had no illusions about what America was really like. But Khalil was still an unknown quantity and he wanted to make sure that he wasn't so corrupted by consumerism and playa fantasies that he could begin a new life without going on a spending spree. When you made a big score, nothing could get you caught faster than throwing your money around. His favorite movie *Dead Presidents*, showed what happened if you did. Temple sighed. He was going to have to read Khalil the riot act.

Entering Juno's love nest, Temple walked straight up to Seidman, who was moaning quietly while holding his bandaged hand.

"Your pain will be over soon, one way or the other," he said ominously. He pulled a syringe out of his bag, rolled up Seidman's left sleeve, and injected him with a huge dose of morphine.

"He won't be saying or doing anything for a long time," Temple said to the four kidnappers, who were seated around a table covered with playing cards, drinks and magazines. "Stop whatever you were doing. It's time to talk about your futures."

Khalil, Rasheeda, Mamadou and Juno turned toward Temple as he pulled up a chair. The large white man faced them with an expression that made him look like a cross between a stern parent and a Mafia hit man.

"The money has been transferred into three separate accounts, one for Mamadou, one for Juno, one for Khalil and Rasheeda. You are all wealthier than you have ever been in your lives. But you are not free to use the money as you please. Everything you do has to be approved by me and the people who work with me."

"What the fuck?" Khalil shouted out as the others gasped. "Who the fuck are you? Rasheeda! What did we get ourselves involved in?"

"Shut up, Khalil, and listen very carefully," Temple said quietly, but in a voice that made everyone's blood turn cold.

"When you called me in to help solve your problem, you became members for life of an organization called the Peoples' Justice Cadre. We are people all over the world, in all walks of life, who do whatever is necessary to even the score between the poor and the rich. We get money to people who need it, neutralize corrupt politicians and police, give people new identities when they are running from the law, and generally make life miserable for racists, dictators and corporate thugs. No one knows who we are. We do everything secretly and we don't take money for what we do so we're impossible to trace."

Rasheeda smiled slyly. She always knew Temple had to have something crazy up his sleeve, she just hoped Khalil could accept it.

"Some of you may have thought I was acting alone, but I have ten different people, some of them in other countries, working to make sure you get your money and that none of you can be linked to Seidman when you start spending it."

Khalil looked over to Mamadou and Juno angrily, but the two of them nodded, too focused on what any money could mean for their families to protest. Even Rasheeda didn't seem surprised or upset. *What the fuck?*

"I have a separate plan for each of you. With the money you now have, you will be able to do things for yourselves and people you care about that you could only dream of before. But the one condition of getting this money is that the hustles you were involved in have to stop immediately. No more drug dealing, no more stealing cars, no more selling spare parts on the black market. You can't do anything to draw the attention of the authorities."

"Are you okay with that?" Temple asked. For Rasheeda, this was a welcome relief—all she ever wanted was to get away from the street hustle.

"Yes!" she said, before turning to stare down the others who had all remained silent. "What the fuck is wrong with you all? You wanted to get out of the ghetto—this is our chance. Gettin' outta the ghetto means no more hustles. What's wrong with y'all?"

"The little chica's right. This is the only way," Juno said.

"Yes," all of them said in unison, albeit Khalil and Doo with little enthusiasm.

"I hope you mean what you're saying, because if you betray the PJC and go back to doing what you did before, I may have to have you killed."

A collective gasp rose from Khalil and Mamadou. Juno had been around long enough not to be surprised.

"Here's the plan. Mamadou, you will access your two million dollar account directly through me. I understand you want to buy the building your father's store is in and set up an import-export business for African grocery stores all over the Bronx. The PJC will be proud to help you make your vision a reality. We have people who can work with you from the African side and we have people here who work in real estate. Within the next two years, all these things will happen provided you stay in school and get your business degree. Are you down with us?"

Mamadou rose to shake Temple's hand. "Assalaam alaikum, Professor Temple. May Allah bless you," he said, his voice now strong. "I will do anything you ask if it will help my father and other African immigrants gain control of their businesses."

"As for you Juno, you will have the same arrangement as Mamadou, your account will be accessed through me. I understand you want to purchase the coastal area in your village in Honduras so that developers can't displace your family. I am already in touch with people in Honduras to make this happen. We will use half of your funds to do that, the other half will be used to upgrade the equipment in your garage so you will have the best truck-repair shop in New York City. You will make hundreds of thousands of dollars a year without having to dismantle another stolen car. Are you down with this?"

"Si, Professor Temple, gracias," Juno replied with a worried look on his face. "Mi gente can now own the land they have always lived on. But what if the developers try to get them off with guns rather than money?"

"I wouldn't worry about that Juno," Temple said. "The PJC in Honduras will be paying them a visit in the next few days and making them an offer they can't refuse. They won't go near your family."

"As for you Khalil and Rasheeda, it's a little trickier—you are the direct connect to Seidman."

Rasheeda grabbed Khalil's hand. There was a worried look all over her face as Temple continued sternly.

"The PCJ has decided that you will be located to a place outside the

United States, where you will begin new lives. But in the meantime, you will be moving out of your apartments into safe houses while my associates move your families to new apartments in the North Bronx and make sure that the children there are enrolled in good schools. Are you okay with that?"

"Yes, Professor Temple. Thank you soo much!" Rasheeda replied.

Khalil remained silent while Rasheeda stroked his arm, willing him to say something, anything. His face was an expressionless mask.

"Good. In the next five minutes, a car will come for Rasheeda and Khalil will come with me. After I take care of business with Rasheeda and Khalil, I will return to deal with Seidman. In the meantime, Mamadou and Juno watch him and give him some painkillers if he seems uncomfortable."

"We're on it," said Mamadou, now completely convinced that Temple meant every word that he said.

"Now, it's time to break up the gang. Juno and Mamadou, you won't be seeing Khalil and Rasheeda for many years, so say your good-byes."

The four kidnappers proceeded to exchange hugs, tears streaming down their faces. The excitement, as well as the fear, brought forth powerful emotions in all, except for Khalil, who stood dejected and silent.

A horn rang outside.

"Okay Rasheeda. That's for you."

Rasheeda grabbed Khalil fiercely, tears still streaming down her eyes.

"Just have faith," she said softly.

Turning quickly, Rasheeda went up the stairs, where Temple's secretary, Rosa, was waiting for her in a Lincoln town car she had rented. Rosa, a beautiful Puerto Rican woman who rocked an Afro and had seen more in her thirty years than most people had in two lifetimes, was going to take Rasheeda to Temple's apartment where she would be staying, under the care of Temple and his life partner, Clarice, for the next week. Rosa, whose glamorous exterior belied her training as a professional kick-boxer, would also be in charge of relocating Rasheeda's mother and sister in a new apartment on Gun Hill Road near Montifiore Hospital. If anybody fucked with her, Temple knew, they would get the same treatment as the two girls who tried to jump her outside her project apartment. Both were knocked out cold.

CHAPTER **36**

Two minutes later, Temple motioned to Khalil and the two men trudged up the stairs to Temple's CRV, where Temple held the door open so that Khalil could take the front seat. That is, after Temple cleared off the papers, crumbs and cups that cluttered the car.

Temple drove the car up to Hunts Point Avenue, crossing under the Bruckner and turning right onto Faile Street, where a row of six-story apartment buildings stood across from some newly built, shoddily constructed townhouses, which passed as luxury for Bronx's poor.

"Okay young man, it's time I told it to you straight," Temple said, facing Khalil's surprised face. "I love Rasheeda like she was my own daughter, and there isn't anything I won't do for her. But I don't know you and I really don't trust you."

"Hey man," Khalil started before Temple lifted up one hand to silence him.

Temple continued, "I am about to set the two of you up with good jobs in a city in Canada, where everyone has housing and medical care and enough to eat. You are going to be thinking you ended up in paradise, and will be surrounded by good-looking women of every color and shade, who will be all over a brother like you."

Temple then put a huge hand on Khalil's shoulder and squeezed hard. Khalil felt the rage rise up in him, but remembered what he had seen Temple do to Seidman and forced himself not react.

"You are going be tempted like you never have been tempted, but if I find out you are cheating on Rasheeda, I am going to follow you up there, cut off your dick and carry it on a stick through the streets of the Bronx!"

Temple squeezed harder. It took everything Khalil had not to scream. He couldn't believe how strong this white man was.

"Do you hear me?"

"Yes, Professor Temple!" Khalil blurted out.

Temple released his vise-like grip "Now give me your gun," he told Khalil. Khalil hesitated—he hadn't been without a gun in years.

Temple nodded, acknowledging Khalil's discomfort. "Where you are going, you won't be needing it anymore."

Khalil took out his .38 and handed it to Temple, who picked up his cell phone and sent out a text message.

All of a sudden, a built Black man in his twenties wearing a dark blue Ecko sweatshirt walked up to the car and got in the back seat. When Khalil turned around, he looked into the eyes of a man who clearly had walked the same streets and seen many of the same things that Khalil did.

"Khalil, meet Jeremiah Little," Temple said. "He's going to be taking care of you for the next few weeks. Jeremiah may look like a street nigga, and still lives on the block where he was born, but he teaches sociology at Columbia and is hands-down the best student I've taught in the last ten years. Besides, Rasheeda, that is."

"What up, brother?" Jeremiah said, giving his fist to Khalil for a bump.

"A'ight, my brother," Khalil responded, suddenly feeling relaxed for the first time in weeks. Beneath the tough exterior, there was a kindness in Jeremiah's eyes that put Khalil at ease. Maybe he could let his guard down and actually talk to this brother the way he talked to Rasheeda.

"You'll be staying with me 'til you leave the country," Jeremiah told Khalil. "While you're in my crib, I will be moving your mother, brothers, sister, and her children to a new apartment in a safe neighborhood and setting up an escrow account so the rent, phone, and electric are paid automatically every month. You won't have to worry about them getting evicted."

"What if my mother starts drinking again?" Khalil said, picturing the state she was in the last time he was home. It had only been a few days, but after everything they had been through, it seemed like a lifetime. "Who will make sure the kids go to school?"

"I have a friend up there who will be looking in on them three or four times a week. The kids are going to be put in good schools and get all the tutoring they need. You can leave the country knowing they are going to have the best of everything."

Jeremiah held up his fist for Khalil to bump again. "On that, you have my word."

"Brother that sounds great," Khalil said. Suddenly, his body became tense again. "But what about my connect? I can't disappear on him without him sending someone to track me down."

"I'll take care of that," Temple said. "After I deal with Seidman, I am going to pay José a little visit and give him a $10,000 severance payment, after some of my associates take his girlfriend hostage for a few hours. He'll cooperate."

"As you can see," Jeremiah told Khalil with a little laugh, "Professor Temple is a very persuasive person. You won't believe some of the things he did to get me to become a professor. But he never, ever lied to me, and he won't lie to you. Professor Temple's word is truly his bond. Now, come with me, brother, your new life is about to begin."

Khalil got out of the car and looked back at Temple. He saw something new on Temple's face, a hint of a kindness and compassion that he had never seen in the man before.

"Good luck, Khalil. I hope you turn out to be the man that Rasheeda thinks you are. You have a great example in Jeremiah. Listen, learn, and take advantage of everything you have been given and use it to help people in need. If you stay on the right path, the PJC will always protect you, and I will always have your back."

"Thank you, Professor Temple," Khalil said, "I appreciate you believing in Rasheeda and me."

CHAPTER **37**

Temple looked at the two young men walking together and smiled. Maybe this would work. Maybe the most talented people in the hood would begin coming together to build up their communities, rather than competing with one another for ill-begotten wealth.

Now the tough part of the day had come: dealing with Seidman. And it wasn't even two p.m. yet.

Temple drove back to the garage with a heavy heart. There was a part of him that wanted Seidman to live. Temple had the contacts to set him up running an oceanfront resort and casino for Hugo Chavez in Venezuela, a job Seidman would be good at, and which would him keep out of the hands of the U.S. authorities. But he also knew that Seidman would never forgive him for dissolving his finger and that he had powerful underworld contacts who helped him set up his secret accounts. The last thing Temple and the PJC needed was a war with a criminal organization as strong and ruthless as they were—a war he knew neither group could really win.

No, Seidman had to die.

Temple parked by Juno's garage and headed down to the room where he found Seidman moaning in his chair. Juno and Mamadou were watching him carefully. Temple pulled out his syringe, filled it to the brim with morphine and injected Seidman with the solution. Then, he did the same thing two more times, until he had given a Seidman a fatal dose.

"The poor guy will never know what hit him," Temple told Mamadou and Juno "And he certainly won't feel what we are going to do to him now."

Temple, Mamadou and Juno waited in silence while the morphine did its work. In five minutes, Seidman was dead.

"Do you have a pickup truck in the garage?" Temple asked Juno.

"*Claro, mi amigo*, I have several."

"Get the largest one you have and fill it with garbage. Then give us the signal and we will carry Seidman up packed in two garbage bags. I will take care of the rest."

While Juno loaded the truck, Mamadou and Temple put Seidman's corpse in two large black garbage bags and sealed them together with tape. When Juno gave the signal, Mamadou and Temple carried up their package and threw it in the back of a large black Ford pickup filled with identical black bags.

"I'll take over from here," Temple said.

With a grim expression, Temple drove the truck toward one of the twenty waste transfer stations that sat in the Hunt's Point and Mott Haven sections of the Bronx. Here, garbage was turned into solid waste that was sent by barge or truck to states like Virginia, but not before leaving the South Bronx residents with the highest asthma rate in the world.

A friend of Temple's opened the gate and escorted him to a huge conveyer belt, which carried garbage into a giant machine that chopped it up into a thick soupy mass. It made a terrible noise and emitted a worse smell. They unloaded the thirty-odd black garbage bags onto the belt and watched until they chugged into the mouth of the machine.

R.I.P., Robert Seidman, Temple said to himself. Finally your money is being put to good use.

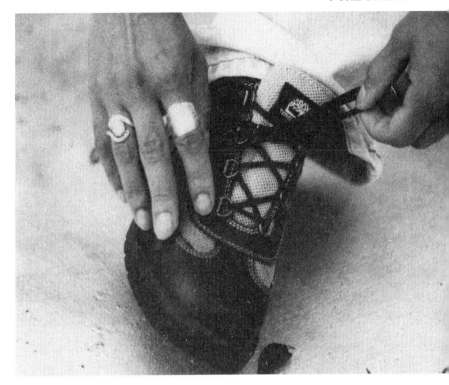

CHAPTER **38**

Khalil followed Jeremiah up the two flights of stairs to his apartment, noticing the explosive force with which he propelled his two-hundred-pound body upward.

This nigga's got some strong legs Khalil thought as he bounded up after Jeremiah.

"Where'd you say you teach?" he asked as they approached the apartment door

"Columbia," Jeremiah replied. "It's on the West Side of Manhattan, not too far from Harlem. I'm also a student there, so you might say I am getting on-the-job training. I teach and go to school at the same time."

"Damn, nigga," Khalil said, as Jeremiah put the key in the door. "I never had no teachers like you when I was in school. Or like Temple for that matter. You more like thugs than professors!"

"No reason someone can't be both," Jeremiah said as has he opened the door to a large, airy apartment, filled with more books than Khalil had ever seen in his life. "We're starting a new trend. Maybe you can follow in our footsteps. If you like college, maybe you can go on to graduate school and become a professor. It beats working for a living and is definitely more fun than selling drugs. Take it from me. I've done both."

"I hear you, my brother, but I'm definitely gonna have to step up my reading," Khalil said, taking note of the books that were piled on tables in every room, including the kitchen and bathroom, and filled bookcases in Jeremiah's bedroom, living room and the hallway linking the two. The only place he saw that remotely resembled this was Jihad's cell at Coxsackie. "Have you read all these books?" Khalil asked.

Jeremiah nodded his head in agreement, motioning Khalil to have a seat on his worn black couch.

Moving some books to the floor beside him, Khalil sat taking it in. "Damn nigga, how do you find the time to eat? How do you find time to sleep? How do you find time to fuck?"

"At school, they call what I do 'multitasking,'" Jeremiah said, moving swiftly to the kitchen and producing two Heinekens, before pulling up a chair across from Khalil. "I can read and eat at the same time. I read when I go to the bathroom, and I always keep a book at the side of my bed when I'm sleeping. The one thing I draw the line on is fucking. I never read when I'm fucking!"

"Thank God," Khalil said laughing as he opened the beer with his teeth. "I don't think Rasheeda would be very happy if I was reading a book when I was going down on her."

"No, Khalil, I don't recommend that," Jeremiah said, laughing as well. "But you have a full week that you will be spending with me and that would be the perfect time to get some reading done as we're going to have to keep you under wraps until you leave for Canada. It will be a good way to prepare yourself for the college courses Temple is going to enroll you in."

"Me in college?" Khalil said, shaking his head. "Who would believe that? Certainly not my teachers. Not the Bloods around Patterson who brought me into the drug game."

"Hey Khalil, somewhere along the line, some brother awakened you to the power of your own mind. Otherwise, you wouldn't be with a sister like Rasheeda. And Temple would be smacking you down or taking you out, not setting up college courses for you."

"Yeah, a brother named Jihad did that when I was upstate. But even he would be surprised at where I am headed."

"Well, educate yourself. You're smart enough to handle anything that comes your way. Some niggas would die for the opportunity you are being granted."

"I hear that," Khalil said. "But can I rest a little before I start reading? I need to relieve some of the stress I've been under. Kidnapping that Seidman nigga was not easy. I would love to hear some music, and if you've got a blunt to smoke that would be even better."

"I've got just what the doctor ordered," Jeremiah said, disappearing into his bedroom as Khalil sat on the couch next to a huge bookcase filled with books on Black history, and novels and memoirs written by Black authors, some he even recognized. On the wall across from the bookcase were posters of Malcolm X, Marcus Garvey and Nelson Mandela. Returning with a blunt, Jeremiah lit it, and passed it to Khalil while he connected his iPod to a small sound system sitting on the bookcase.

Soon, haunting beats came out of the speakers, and accompanying words that sent chills through Khalil's body.

> *Behind enemy lines, my niggas is cellmates*
> *Most of the youth never escape the jail fate*
> *Super maximum camps will advance they game plan*
> *To keep us in the hands of the man locked up*

As the smoke took effect, and as the stories in the song kept building to a climax, for the first time Khalil had a clear vision of where his life might be headed. Like the brothers who wrote the song, he might get a chance to speak for, and fight for, all the niggas he grew up around who were trapped in poverty. And who were doing the Man's work by killing one another while selling their drugs. Khalil had been one of those niggas until Jihad had awakened him, and now he was being given the weapons to act on that knowledge.

> *You ain't gotta be locked up to be in prison*
> *Look how we livin'*
> *30,000 niggas a day, up in the bing, standin' routine*
> *They put us in a box just like our life on the block*
> *Behind enemy lines*

"You all right, Khalil?" Jeremiah asked him when the song ended.

"Jeremiah, I know this ain't gon' sound right, but that song got deep inside me. I want to be able to reach people like that some day."

"With hard work, my brother, you will. But for now, get some rest. I am going to go back to your apartment to pick up your clothes and give a heads up to your mother and sister on what will be happening to them and the kids. On the way back, I will be hitting Mickey D's. What do you want me to get you?"

"A big Mac, two packs of chicken tenders and a large fries. I need to keep my energy up."

"Damn, nigga, that's 3,000 calories right there. Temple would kill me if he knew I were buying you shit like that. On the other hand, I like Mickey D's as much as you do. Fuck it. Let's party!"

"Word, Jeremiah, you my kind of nigga. See you in a few."

Khalil settled back into the couch as Jeremiah closed the apartment door behind him. After a few minutes, he walked over to the bookcase and looked through Jeremiah's collection. He saw names he knew from Jihad's library—Malcolm X, Donald Goines, Iceberg Slim, and Piri Thomas—but he also saw titles and authors he wasn't familiar with, and among those one book seemed to most command his attention. It was called *Street Dreams* by Kwan. He picked it up, looked at the cover, weighed it in his hand, and started reading.

Six hours later, when Jeremiah came through the door with a suitcase full of Khalil's clothes and a huge bag of treats from McDonalds, Khalil hadn't moved from the spot where he was when he had begun reading. Kwan had taken him on a journey so much like his own that he felt he was living the story rather than reading it. If they assigned books like this in his courses, college was going to be a smooth ride.

"So, I see you found something that interested you," Jeremiah said with a smile.

"Interested ain't the half, my brother. This Kwan nigga speaks pure truth. If you got more books like this, the time 'til my flight out is going to seem like a couple hours."

"Don't worry, Khalil, there's at least ten books just as good as that sitting on the shelf. Think of yourself as taking a course at Street University. Now put that shit down, and let's eat. I'm starving."

"That works for me," Khalil said as he followed Jeremiah into the kitchen.

There he put the food down on a wooden table half covered with books and newspapers. Jeremiah got out a couple of sodas from the fridge and the two men greedily devoured their hamburgers, fries and chicken tenders. Jeremiah smothered everything he ate with ketchup, and Khalil used pepper and salt. After twenty minutes of hard-core eating, during which neither man said a word, Khalil decided to ask Jeremiah something that had been weighing on his mind.

"Jeremiah, no offense, but you seem to be a street nigga just like me. How did you get through all this shit without getting killed, sent upstate, or thrown out of school? Did you have parents who looked after you or some shit like that?"

"No, Khalil, I came very close to getting pulled into the life. My father was never in the picture and my mother, who was the smartest person I ever met until I took a course with Temple, became a crack-head when I was eight. By ten, I was running the streets, holding drugs for the crews on Faile Street, and starting to mess up in school."

"That sounds just like me!" Khalil said. "Only it was a gang, not a crew, that pulled me in."

"See, we didn't have gangs on Faile Street. We had street crews that were in competition with one another, so there were shoot-outs all the time, which was even more dangerous. But anyway, back to my story. When my mother hit rock bottom, my grandmother, who was a Jamaican lady raised in Belize, decided to take me and my sister in, and from that point on everything changed."

"How come?"

"The first thing my grandmother did was whip my ass. The second thing was to put me in Catholic school. And when they tested me there, they found that even though I was in third grade, I was reading on a sixth-grade level. Once my grandmother heard how smart I was, that was the end of my street life. Every spare minute, she was taking me to the zoo, to the museum, to the library. She enrolled me in after-school programs for sports, even if it meant taking me to the other side of the Bronx."

"How did the niggas on your block respond to that? Did they just let you become an herb without giving you all kinds of shit?"

"Well, couple things. First of all, I still snuck out the house enough to be part of the drug biz. I didn't hold drugs or sell drugs, but I was a lookout. Some of that I could do from the street, some from the window of my apartment. I had a great eye for Five-O. I could tell a cop from a mile away, no matter what car they be driving or how they dressed. I was probably the best lookout on Faile Street. But second, there was an old hustler on Faile Street named Lionel that everybody still looked up to even though he was long out of the business. Lionel had spent ten years upstate for murder and that carried a lot of weight, even among the young guns. And Lionel decided to look out for me. He had learned the value of education when he was in prison and he decided that I was the person on the block who was going to make it and make everyone proud. So, he told all the drug crews to give me a free pass. But that wasn't all. He used to buy me books and then sit down and discuss them with me on the benches across the street. It was Lionel, even more than my high school teachers, who gave me the critical reading skills that allowed me to excel in college. The brother was like an encyclopedia, but he also knew how to look at things from more than one point of view."

"Damn, nigga, so instead of being pulled down by the hood, you was saved by the hood."

"Exactly so, my brother," Jeremiah said. "No one can really save us but ourselves, which is why I am so excited to have a street soldier like you become part of PJC. Someone like you can reach the most hard-core brothers and sisters because you've lived what they're going through and walked the walk."

Jeremiah put his fist out and Khalil bumped it.

"My brother, I know you've had a hard life, and that what awaits you isn't easy, but there is no feeling in the world like joining with other street niggas to fight for justice for our people. You'll see. We're going to make history together."

"I believe you, my brother," Khalil said. "I believe you. Now, let's have more of that good weed before we make any more history!"

CHAPTER **39**

As Rasheeda sat in the car next to Rosa on the way to her safe house, she felt overwhelmed by emotion. She couldn't believe everything that had happened in the past few days between kidnapping Seidman and bringing in Temple. Staring out the window at the passing Bronx, Rasheeda still couldn't even accept that something had actually worked out for her. From having to leave Harlem at age eight, to defending herself in the Bronx, to dealing with her mother's drinking and the birth of Junior, sometimes she felt like the deck was stacked against her. Even the good things in her life—getting into Lehman and getting with Khalil—weren't worry free. Lehman had meant stripping, and watching Khalil struggle to get out was almost as bad as her own problems.

"You okay?" Rosa said, noticing Rasheeda's silence.

"I just can't believe everything that happened."

Rosa nodded.

"And now, I don't even know where I'm going, even for the next week much less the rest of my life. This shit is crazy," Rasheeda continued.

"Don't worry. Temple's got your back. It's all gonna be okay. Better than okay."

Rasheeda nodded, continuing to watch Bronx's streets go by until pretty soon they were in Manhattan and finally, Brooklyn.

"Rosa! Where are you taking me?"

"It's a surprise."

As they pulled up to Nelson Temple's brownstone, Rasheeda spirits began to rise. Especially when she saw Clarice walk outside. Dressed in black pants, a bright red, velvet, long-sleeved top, large hoop earrings and a multicolored scarf, Clarice was a woman who still turned heads. Her coppered-colored skin was beautifully set off with long gray hair. Rasheeda jumped out of the car and gave Clarice a big hug. Rasheeda thought she would never see her again.

"Hey, sweetie," Clarice said. "Temple thought you might want to stay here while he made your arrangements."

Rasheeda nodded, tears welling up in her eyes from the emotion and stress of the last few days.

"Come on, let's get you inside."

Leading Rasheeda into the small, but tastefully decorated apartment, Clarice sat Rasheeda down on the couch before bustling into the kitchen. Soon enough, she had returned with heated plates of fried catfish, black-eyed peas, green beans and peach cobbler.

"Damn, Clarice," Rasheeda said hungrily, looking over the spread.

"They just some leftovers," Clarice said, sitting next to her on the soft green suede couch. "Now, eat up. You need your strength."

As the two women ate their fill, Rasheeda filled Clarice in on the details of the kidnapping, and her mixed emotions of both fear and excitement for the future.

"Do you know where Khalil and I are going to end up?" Rasheeda asked.

"It's not final, but I think so."

"Where?"

"I can't tell you yet, but I think you're gonna love it."

"I just can't believe that I'm finally outta Cheetah's, outta the projects, outta my mother's house. Clarice, is it bad that I'm happy to be away from my mother?"

"Rasheeda," Clarice said, taking her hand and looking straight into her eyes. "You have done everything a mother could ever have asked for and more, especially considering your life. Now, I know you feel responsible to take care of Junior, but it's time for you to take care of yourself."

"But what if something happens to Junior?" Rasheeda said sadly.

"It's not gonna. Temple's going make sure your mom gets some help, just like Khalil's family. Now," Clarice continued, raising one eyebrow, "when are we gonna get to the important topic? Tell me about your man."

Rasheeda felt her cheeks blush as a wide smile full of pride came across her face.

"Hmm-hmm," Clarice said. That good, huh? Spill."

"Well, of course the man is one handsome brother. He's tall and built with dark skin like mines. And then, he's got this sexy scar on his right side. It just adds a dangerous sexy flavor to his look. Not too pretty, a real man—you know what I'm saying?"

"Uh-huh, I do. Nelson's got a really bad scar on his stomach, but don't tell him I told you. Stroking it sometimes just reminds you of what our men go through, what they fight for."

"Yeah," Rasheeda said, thinking about Khalil's dedication to his family. It was definitely gonna be hard for him to be away from them.

"So, how did your man get his scar?"

"In prison. They send him upstate as a juvie for dealin'."

"Yeah, and how do you feel about that?"

"What the prison or the dealing?"

Clarice laughed. "Now don't get sassy with me—both!"

Rasheeda paused to ponder the question. Almost everyone she knew growing up had been involved in illegal activity, whether buying or selling in the drug game or some other sort of hustle.

"I never really thought about it," she said.

"Really? A smart, ambitious girl like you?"

"Yeah, but when that's all you know, why would you expect any man you fall in love with to have a legit job or no prison record."

"That's sad, girl. Sad."

"It is, but even so, Khalil's different."

"Hmm. How's that?"

Rasheeda stared into her lap. "He's smart, you know? Not just street smart, either. I can talk to him about school and he gets it. He used to be great at school before the Bloods got him into trouble. In prison, he got his GED and everything, but you know how it is on the outside if you got a prison record."

"Hmm-hmm."

Raising her gaze to meet Clarice's, she smiled. "And he's loyal. Real loyal. He's not like any other man I know, except maybe Temple. Khalil would never betray me for a sack chaser or abandon his family to get ahead. You know, not having my father around or any man that didn't walk away or two-time, that means something."

"For sure," Clarice smiled, glad to see Rasheeda in good hands. "I mean that's what I see in Temple. You know, we've been together a long time. And I'm not from these parts; I'm from Georgia. So when I first met him, I thought he was street, and hard-core, and maybe I couldn't deal with some of the things he felt he had to do or had done. Nelson Temple may be a professor now, but that man's no saint. He's done some things in his life that would make Khalil's crimes seem like jaywalking."

"And you're okay with that too?"

"I wasn't at first, but then I thought to myself—would you rather have a man so loyal and honest that it drives him to break the law, maybe hurt someone here or there, or a man like Seidman—a successful, supposedly upstanding citizen who feels the need to go to a strip club up in the Bronx. Loyalty's a rare thing for men but it's what I needed. So yeah, I'm okay with that."

Rasheeda gave Clarice a big hug. "Yeah, me too. I love Khalil."

"A'ight then! Then let's bring out the wine 'cuz I want to hear the real details," Clarice said, rising to put away the plates.

Rasheeda giggled. "What do you mean?"

"Oh, you know what I mean," Clarice winked from the kitchen. "How is it?"

Rasheeda stood up, carrying the remaining plates into the kitchen.

"Girl, you have no idea. That man, my man, well, he definitely got some special skills."

CHAPTER **40**
THREE MONTHS LATER

Khalil sat on the park bench overlooking the Canadian bay. He was tired from the three hours he spent refereeing basketball in the youth center. Except for the little Asian point guard, who was as quick as anyone he had ever seen in a Bronx schoolyard, the players on the court all sucked. All they wanted to do was knock each other into the wall and fight like it was a fucking hockey game. Bronx niggas were tough, but at least they had skills. And they didn't fight just to break someone's nose and then be their best friend. In the Bronx, when you started a fight, you better be prepared to kill, or die, because if the person who you were fighting wasn't packing, their cousin, uncle or best friend was. You didn't shake hands when it was over—because it was never over. Shit could go on for years.

Khalil looked around him and shook his head. In his wildest dreams, he never thought a place like this existed: streets so clean you could eat off the sidewalks, flowers hanging from baskets in City Parks. People always smiling, and a whole bunch of them openly high. You could carry up to a pound of pot up here and never get arrested if you didn't try to sell it.

But the thing that got to Khalil the most was the way the people mixed. I mean, it wasn't like Khalil wasn't used to different colors because you had it all and more in the Bronx with the Spanish-speaking peoples and Africans, but here you had white people hanging out with people from every color of the rainbow, not just playing ball and partying with them, but marrying them and starting families. It seemed like everybody was fucking everybody else in Canada, not in secret or in the back room of a strip club, but in the broad light of day. Shit, every day, another beautiful woman was sweating him, promising to give him a piece of heaven if he let them suck his dick. White girls, Asian girls, Samoan girls, Native American girls, Brazilian girls, African girls and everything in between. Because he had Rasheeda, the most beautiful girl in the whole country, and because he remembered what Temple had told him, he wasn't buying, but damn, it sure was tempting.

Sometimes, Khalil thought he was going crazy! How did he end up going from the South Bronx to Victoria, British Columbia—the cruise-ship capital of the Canadian coast?

He looked at the all the fat white people getting off the cruise ships on their way back from Alaska, spending money like it was no tomorrow, stuffing their fat asses and bellies with food, and he thought of what would happen if a cruise ship docked in the South Bronx and tourists started walking through Patterson Houses on their way to the hub. Every last one of them would be mugged, not just for their money, but just for the chance to give them a beat down.

Which is exactly what Khalil wanted to do. He took one look at the fat white Americans and wanted to give them a beat down to avenge all the people he grew up with who would never set foot on a cruise ship and never walk the streets of a foreign city like they owned it. He wanted to snatch their purses and steal their wallets and send them sprawling to the ground with their clothes ripped and blood pouring from their mouths

But who was Khalil kidding? He was now a whole lot richer than most of the people he wanted to mug. He had everything he ever wanted in life, the girl of his dreams living with him in a beautiful two-bedroom apartment, enough money to buy anything he wanted, a legal job paying more than he had made selling drugs, and a chance to take classes at a community college and eventually get a college degree. He should have been happy, but something was missing and he was afraid to think about what it was.

Could it have been his youth in poverty?

Could it have been rage?

Could it have been fear that he was going to die any moment?

Was Khalil addicted to the ghetto and the survivor's pride he felt every day walking the streets of the Bronx?

Every day, everyone who saw him knew he was bad. Because a brother couldn't walk with confidence through the streets of the South Bronx without a crew the way Khalil did unless they were seriously BAD.

But in Victoria everyone walked around like they didn't have a care in the world. And why not? Everyone had medical care. Everyone had a place to live. Everyone had food. There were no ghettoes. There were no slums.

He should have loved being here, but he didn't.

And worse yet, other than his teacher, mentor and new best friend, Jamal Joseph, the ex-Black Panther at the community college that Professor Temple had hooked him up with, there was nobody he could talk to about this. They would all think he was crazy for missing the Bronx.

Even Rasheeda. She loved everything about her new life. She loved being back in college. She loved her job as a restaurant manager. She loved not having money worries. But above all, she loved being free of the strip club and the almost daily humiliation of being groped and fondled and sexually assaulted by men.

She was his queen, the one part of his life that he would do nothing to change, and he wouldn't say or do anything to make her unhappy.

Khalil got up from the bench and began walking along the water to the high-rise apartment building where he and Rasheeda now lived. He walked through the unlocked entrance, through a spotlessly clean lobby, and took the elevator to the sixteenth floor. Instinctively, he found himself looking over his shoulder for the Patterson Bloods and bracing himself for the smell of pee. He found neither. The elevator smelled like a flower shop.

He walked to the door of his apartment, opened it with his key, and saw Rasheeda, wearing jeans and a spectacularly beautiful blouse with Native American imagery, putting flowers on the dining room table. She glowed with beauty and happiness. She ran to him and gave him a big hug.

"Oh, Khalil, I love it here so much. Thank you for bringing me here! Thank you for making my life so wonderful."

"Boo, I would do anything for you," Khalil said, cheering up immediately "You're my reason for living, my Ghetto Queen, the most beautiful sister, the world has ever seen."

As Khalil's spirits lifted, so did something else. As he pressed himself against Rasheeda, he felt himself getting hard.

"Ooh, what do we have here?" Rasheeda said, reaching down and grabbing his sex. "That's a dangerous condition. We have to do something to reduce the swelling."

Rasheeda pulled him to the bedroom, pulled down his jeans, and sucked on him greedily while Khalil moaned with pleasure. Then Khalil returned the favor, and brought her to a climax with his lips and tongue.

An hour later, the couple lay pressed against each other, exhausted but happy, looking out the window at the ships moving through the bay.

"I can't believe we're here, Khalil. I really thought we were going to die in the hood, or worse yet, turn into our parents. But now we're getting all the opportunities in life—an education, good jobs, and a chance to live without fear. I wish we could lift a magic wand and give everyone in the Bronx this opportunity."

"We have no magic wand, baby. Look what it took for us to get out. We're lucky we're not dead or in jail. The odds are stacked against people like us. It took a miracle—and Professor Temple—to get us where we are today."

"I know, boo. But someday, we have to pay Professor Temple back. And not in money—we have to help someone the way he helped us."

Khalil turned and kissed Rasheeda deeply. "I'm so glad you said that Rasheeda, because as great as it is for us here, it doesn't feel like home. Someday, I'm going to need to get back to the Bronx and make things right."

"Baby, I know what you're saying, but I can't go back, at least not yet. I can't face being anywhere near that strip club or anywhere nearby for that matter. It's too hard. Maybe in five years, maybe ten. Then we can do it right."

Khalil's spirits sank. He didn't know if he could last another five years away from the Bronx. But he wasn't going to tell Rasheeda that. He wasn't going to say anything to make her unhappy.

"You're right, boo." Khalil said, finally. "All in good time. I'm going to head off to the college and see Professor Joseph. Have a great night at the restaurant. I'll see you when you get home."

Khalil kissed Rasheeda on the forehead, slipped on his jeans and shirt and went downstairs to the bike rack in the basement of his building. He took out his bike and rode the two miles to the community college, passing as many people on bikes as he saw in cars. In the Bronx, people would have run those bike riders off the road.

Khalil parked his bike, walked up the steps of the college and turned down the hall, passing students who reflected the typical mixture of the city—white, Asian, Native American, Black, Samoan, and everything in between. No one congregated in groups divided by race. No one looked angry.

Khalil knocked on his advisor's door and a tall, light-skinned black man with a salt-and-pepper afro let him in with a smile and gave him a bone-crushing hug. The man was just as big as Professor Temple and if anything, even stronger. God knows what the two of them could have done when they were Khalil's age. God knows what they did do!

"So how are you, my brother?" Professor Joseph asked. "Feeling any better about being here? Do you still miss the Bronx? Don't tell me, I know the answer."

"Professor Joseph, I can't hide a thing from you. You see right through me. But tell me, don't you still miss Oakland?"

"Every day, my brother, even though it's been forty years. And I will miss it until the day I die, even though I love Canada, and love my Canadian brothers and sisters. But when you've grown up in the hood and become a ghetto soldier who has had to fight every day to survive, it gets in your blood. Nothing can replace the rush. Nothing can replace the fear. Nothing can replace the feeling that you have survived things that would kill most people and become, to quote from our brothers forced to fight in Vietnam, the baddest motherfucker in the valley."

"So you'll never be able to go back, Professor Joseph?"

"Not until they get rid of the statute of limitations on murder. There are three dead police informers in our Panther chapter that they think I was responsible for."

"Were you?" Khalil said, his eyes widening.

"To quote Malcolm X, '…those who say, don't know, and those who know, don't say.' But what about you? You can go back. What are you going to do?"

"I don't know, Professor Joseph," Khalil said, tapping his fingertips on the edge of the chair. "Rasheeda is incredibly happy here, and I won't do anything to upset her. But to tell you the truth, I see my future back in the Bronx. Once I get my college degree, that's where I'm going to go. That's where the kids need me the most. That's where I will feel most at home. But that may be five, ten years away."

"You're a great student, Khalil. You're going to get your degree way before that."

"I know, Professor Joseph, but I can't move back to the Bronx until Rasheeda is ready and that will take a long time."

"I hear you, Khalil," the giant professor said with a smile. "A woman like Rasheeda comes only once in a lifetime. And she deserves a brother like you. But I may have a solution to your problem."

"And what would that be?" Khalil said, finally steadying his hand in anticipation.

"I'll tell you when the time comes, but don't be surprised if the PJC sends you back to the Bronx to teach a developer or corrupt politician a lesson, or to help a family in trouble. Would you accept such a mission?"

"Hell yes! I am ready right now."

"Be patient, my brother. We are not sending you anywhere until you complete at least a year of college. But don't be surprised—that is if you get all A's your first year—if someone taps you on the shoulder and asks you to be a ghetto soldier again, only this time a soldier for justice."

"Power to the People, Brother Joseph."

"Power to the People, Khalil."

CHAPTER **41**

Dressed only in a light blue towel, Rasheeda opened her closet and sighed with pleasure. Gone were her stripper collection of lacy thongs and gaudy panties. This here was the real shit—beautiful full business suits that made her feel a hundred times sexier than parading around naked. Yeah, they would call her a yuppie in the hood—good thing she wasn't in the hood anymore.

Rasheeda picked out a dark gray suit, paired with a lilac shirt and pumps. She wondered what Mr. Robinson from the bank would say to her loan application now. He'd probably be falling all over himself to pull out her chair and impress her. As Rasheeda admired her new look in the full-length mirror of their huge master bedroom, she thought of Khalil. They'd get back there someday, just not yet. Every time Rasheeda thought of the Bronx, her mother, Cheetah's, she felt the self-confidence, the value she was just starting to find in herself, deflate. Even though she stripped to go to school, stripping had broken her down day by day, until it was hard to remember that the grinding and the groping wasn't a statement of her worth.

Taking one last glance at her reflection, Rasheeda smiled and walked into the living room. Even after a month, she couldn't get over their apartment in Victoria, BC. It was twice as big as the one she shared with her mother and Junior. The bathroom was huge with a long vanity table and full bath. Rasheeda had never had a full bath before and loved slipping in after a long day at work. On top of that, an open kitchen overlooked a comfortable living room and dinning area, complete with a large flat screen. When Rasheeda stood in that kitchen cooking while Khalil studied at the table or watched football, she felt like muthafuckin' Martha Stewart. Hey, she was just another bitch who had to do what she had to do to get that paper.

Rasheeda glanced at the clock, saw it was eight forty-five and rushed out the door. She usually didn't have to be at the nearby restaurant until ten a.m., but she wanted to look over the inventory figures Mrs. Marshall had been showing her the other day. Watching and learning how the Marshalls ran Lucea was like a dream come true. Named for the Jamaican city where they grew up, Lucea was a small café and restaurant located just a few minutes from the apartment. At Lucea, Rasheeda had immediately clicked with Mrs. Marshall. Like Rasheeda, Mrs. Marshall was the money woman. She ran the business, kept the books, and did the marketing—and did it so well in fact that the business was named one of Victoria's newest hotspots after just a year. Now in their tenth year, Mr. Marshall was the food man—a talented chef who brought the flavor of the island to every dish and drink they served.

Although business was good, the Marshalls were Temple's age and looking to slow down—which was where Rasheeda came in. If all went well, once she finished her degree in two years, Rasheeda would take over full time. As Rasheeda walked the final block to the restaurant, she licked her lips. But that's not all, she thought to herself. Once she was in charge, she was gonna use the profits and experience from Lucea's to open up her own spot—a tapas bar and cultural center in the downtown area. There, not only would she serve banging food and drinks, but use the space to highlight local talent—bands, artists, photographers, poetry slams. It was gonna be *the* spot.

At nine a.m. Rasheeda walked into Lucea. She even loved her fucking walk. It was so clean in Victoria—instead of dodging liquor bottles and chicken wings, the streets were lined with carefully kept trees and flowers. No one whistled or looked at her differently either. Most of all she loved the diversity. At Camosun College she studied business with over five hundred Aboriginal students and people from over fifty nations. Rasheeda had never even met a real U.S. Native American but up here, even the college had an indigenous name. And while she knew that for Khalil, this made it difficult to get his bearings, for Rasheeda it was different—for once, she didn't feel her skin color glaring out at class. When people asked her where she was from, they seemed genuinely interested versus in the Bronx, it was to see what hood or territory you rep. Blacks were a minority, but with all the other browns and yellows, it just didn't feel that way.

"Hey Paul," she said, waving to the Filipino busboy they had recently hired. "How you feeling? You getting the ropes?"

"No problem. Hey, you heading over to school later?" Paul, who just turned eighteen, was also a freshman at Camosun with an interest in social work. Rasheeda had met him in one of the required writing classes everyone had to take and was impressed with his demeanor. Even though he had no experience working in a restaurant, when she heard he needed a job, she stuck her neck out and now the Marshalls loved him.

"Yeah, I just came in to look over the paperwork and cover the lunch shift for Mrs. Marshall, then I got econometrics." Mostly Rasheeda worked the weekend shifts to leave her to focus on school during the week.

"Econometrics?" Paul said as he continued to put the restaurant in order—sweeping the floors, bringing down the chairs, and wiping the tables. "You business types. I guess that's why you make the big bucks."

"Ha, ha that's right. It's just a fancy term for applying statistics to economic principals. Besides, don't play that game, you know the tips here are fantastic—I'm almost tempted to quit, put on an apron, and pick up some tables myself," Rasheeda said.

Paul giggled, his scrawny five-six body doubling over in laughter. "But then who would fix all of Mara's mistakes?"

Rasheeda laughed back, nodding her head in agreement. Mara was the most senior waitress, having opened the restaurant with the Marshalls. She was also a complete disaster and put in the wrong order at least once or twice a night.

"Just learn the food so you can take the server test," Rasheeda said, heading down to the office. "I'll see you in a bit. Buzz me if you need anything."

For the next two hours, Rasheeda studied the restaurant's profit margins, and did the inventory. She silently checked on the staff to make sure they had all arrived. At noon, Rasheeda went up to the restaurant to supervise, ensuring the quality of the service and that the food stayed at top level. By three p.m. Mrs. Marshall had arrived and Paul and Rasheeda were off on the bus to class.

Finding her usual spot next to Megan Rivers, a member of the Yale First Nation, Rasheeda greeted her with a smile, and said, "Hey girl, how was your weekend?"

"Good—but I need help on this statistics stuff, especially probability,"

"You wanna go to the library after class?"Rasheeda asked, pulling out her textbook.

"Not really," Megan laughed. "But I will! I can't afford to fail this."

"You won't, not with my help," Rasheeda said confidently.

"Hey, by the way, you coming to our powwow next week?"

"What's a powwow?"

"Then you definitely have to come. Don't you have Native Americans in the U.S.?" Megan laughed.

"Yeah, but I don't think they make it to the Bronx too often."

"Well, the Bronx doesn't make it up here too often either."

"True that, true that. Well, don't you worry, Khalil and me, will be your Bronx reps."

As both girls turned to the start of the lecture, Rasheeda felt her heart swell a bit, thinking of KRS-One's album *South Bronx*.

> *South South Bronx!*
> *Yo where my people at?*
> *South South Bronx!*
> *Yo where my heart is at?*
> *South South Bronx!*

> *C'mon let's bring it back*
> *South South Bronx!*

Yeah the Bronx still had her heart, and one day, yeah one day, she'd be back.

CHAPTER **42**

Dear Professor Temple,

    Thank you so much for your last letter—it's so good to hear that Khalil's and my moms are in rehab and doing well. I know that will ease a lot of guilt for Khalil. It definitely helps me worry a little less about Junior. Did you ever know his real name is Anthony? It's a good name—I picked it out for him, but moms was always too drunk to remember and I guess it reminded her too much of the baby she lost, Adam. Let me know when it's safe to write to them, or maybe call them? I was also wondering if Rosa could check in on Monica and Erika. Is Erika still going to school? Did Monica get the money

I left her? I know that loca will never leave the club, but her lil' sis is mad smart. Maybe Rosa could keep an eye out for her, too.

I'm sorry to ask so much, Doc. You and Rosa have done so much for me, but that way it feels like I'm not abandoning the Bronx, even though part of me wants to. Is it bad that I could just live here forever and forget all about Patterson and Mitchell? I mean, I know that's not true but there was nothing good in my life there—deadbeat dad, drunk mother, crack then heroin, stripping. Here, I was never a stripper. I was never nothing. Here, I'm something. I don't wanna be nothing anymore, and thinking back makes it so hard. The only good thing that ever came outta there was Khalil.

Doc, what do I do about Khalil? He's doing great in school and likes his job, but when he's with me, all he wants to do is rep the hood, talk about the Bronx and all I wanna do is forget. I know deep down he wants to go back. I love him so much, I can't imagine life without him, except if we go back. That I can't imagine, that I can't do—I freeze up and start sweating and think about Money Bags and his finger. Doc, I'm scared I'm gonna lose my man. My home, my family I can deal without, but I can't lose my man, too.

Peace and Love,
Rasheeda

Dear Rasheeda,

I gotta keep this short—they made me director of a new institute, which is an administrative nightmare. Poor Rosa and I are up to our heads in budgets, hiring, proposals—I could have used you right now.

Look, don't worry about Khalil. I know exactly where he's coming from. In fact, I grew up just like him out in Chicago, except I was the only white kid in the projects so I had to fight twice as hard. Khalil is used to being angry and now that he doesn't have any reason to, he doesn't know what to do. It's pent-up energy and he feels isolated. For the first time, not being in a rage is normal. But he'll figure it out—I got my people looking out for him and he loves you. I see that more and more every day from his work at school, from what I'm hearing from my people over there. Everything's gonna be okay—I wouldn't let anything happen to my best student.

But enough about Khalil—I want to hear about your school and your studies. The Marshalls say you are a born businesswoman and they're making even more money off their restaurant then ever before.

Just focus on yourself, Rasheeda, you got everything going for you. Don't think about the Bronx if it hurts still, but know we're holding it down here for when you're ready. Your mom's been sober a month now, Erika's doing well—I'm gonna help her transfer to Lehman this year, and Monica got the money, anonymously, of course. Tell Khalil his end is good, too—his sister's got a job at the post office now and his mom is taking care of the kids at home. They're all making A's in school.

I'm here if you need anything.

Temple

Dear Professor Temple,

You don't know how much your words mean to me. I feel like I can finally breathe again knowing what I know about your experience and what Khalil's going through. Hey, now that the whole "episode" is over, isn't time for you to tell me your past? Were you really affiliated with the PANTHERS? From the first time I met you, I always knew you was GANGASTA!! But damn, Temple, you wasn't playin!

School and everything is da bomb! I was studying for a test now, but I thought I'd take a break to write you. (But don't worry there's no way I'm not acing this mofo!) I'm looking into the Urban Studies concentration like you said, but right now I'm focusing on the businesses still. I love them numbers and no doubt I'm definitely going for the MBA. It was soo good to know Khalil's doing well in school, too. I see him studying, but you gotta give a man space sometimes, you know? Let a man be a man.

Which by the way, I think you're right about Khalil. Last weekend, I got Sunday off and we went with some of my Inuit friends from school to see the whales. I know he hates the cruise lines, but it was good for him to see the real people. Temple, to see the huge whales coming up and crashing on the water just made me so thankful to be here again. Who knew that there was a whole world outside the Bronx? I think Khalil is seeing that, too. Give Clarice a hug for me, and a fist-bump to Rosa!

Rasheeda

P.S. How big is Junior now?

Dear Rasheeda,

Junior is 25 lbs now and walking all over the place. Rosa went and visited last Saturday and said the baby's cheeks are full and healthy and he's stopped crying all the time. Rosa also said fist bumps are old school now and to get with the program. Ha! Clarice sent you a care package—she wouldn't let me se what's inside, but let me know if it arrives. Let Khalil know everything is good. It's all good.

I'm glad you went to see the whales—keep exploring, there really is a whole world out there and you only get to be 20 once.

I got institute stuff up to my ears and football players boycotting my classes—so pretty much everything is the same. Good news, though, I got invited to speak at the University of Victoria next year so I'll be up soon. Gonna do my communism in Harlem thing.

Just never stop pushing, R.

Temple

P.S. I'll tell you about my past when we write my memoir. Think about it, R, your African American studies papers were some of the best.

PPS. Happy Birthday—you didn't think I'd forget did you? You'll be getting some extra money in your account. Buy yourself something special and then go blow up the town with your man.

Dear Temple,

$5000!!! Are you CRAZY!! Thank you so much! Khalil and I went shopping and then downtown for dinner and dancing. We went to this place Nautical Nellie's Steak and Seafood—you ever been there? It was off the chain, steak, lobster the works.

But, hell no, you really crazy! You think I can write a book? Do you know how long it took me to write those 10 pages for class?

I can't wait to see you up in the BC. It's not the Bronx, but it's a'ight! I was just thinking the other day about the Bronx. I know it was hard, but I wouldn't be the gangsta I am, tearing it up in Canada if it weren't for the Bronx. Sure, it was hell, but that's what made me who I am right? Def. 100% Pure Bronx all the way. Hey hey!

Peace,

Rasheeda

EPILOGUE

The call finally came on a Sunday night. Khalil had been waiting for it ever since his transcript arrived at the house with A's in every course. Temple had promised him a mission if he aced all his courses and as Khalil had learned, that nigga always kept his promises.

"Take the bus to Vancouver and get the first flight to JFK," Temple had told him. "Bring enough clothes for four days, including clothes you don't mind getting ripped or stained. We'll give you whatever else you need."

Khalil felt a tingle in his stomach as he tried to imagine what Temple had in store for him. He hated to admit it, but he welcomed the chance to do something dangerous. Danger had been a daily part of Khalil's life since he had first left his apartment in Patterson by himself. It had been there for him in middle school, there for him in high school, there for him in Spofford, there for him in Coxsackie, there for him in every drug deal and beef and it had turned into something between an addiction and an old friend. As much as he loved living with Rasheeda in the most beautiful city in Canada, as much as he loved learning all the things about Black history he had never been taught in school, he missed the rush of being a street soldier in the Bronx. The chance to get that back, even for a few days, filled him with excitement.

The great thing about Rasheeda was that she knew this about him, too. She knew that if she was going to hold onto Khalil, she would have to let him return to the Bronx to help Temple settle old scores. Otherwise, he would want to move back permanently, which she definitely didn't want to do. She just hoped he returned in one piece. The Bronx was like a drug to Khalil, and she didn't mind him indulging once or twice a year, if it made living with him in Canada easier and less stressful.

Khalil packed his bags, boarded the bus to Vancouver and made the plane to JFK with a couple of hours to spare. He had a book that he knew would hold his attention for the six-hour flight—Nathan McCall's *Make Me Wanna Holler*, a classic street tale from the early '90's that still got respect in the joint, and the hood.

He was also looking forward to talking with Jeremiah Little. who had single-handedly relocated his family to an apartment in Norwood, right near Moshulu Parkway. Little kept his two younger brothers, Keyshawn and Kenyatta, on point, and most importantly, off the streets. He enrolled them in after-school programs that taught martial arts, hip-hop poetry, and break dancing. Jeremiah was going to meet him at the airport.

Khalil got off the plane feeling calm, but hyper alert, the same way he felt walking to the mess hall upstate. He had slept nearly five of the six hours on the plane, and was ready for the business at hand. His baggage was carry-on, and as he rolled his leather case down the walkway to the airport exit, he saw Jeremiah standing next to a huge blond-haired man with a beard, who was wearing a loose-fitting shirt and jeans. He was at least two inches taller than Jeremiah and four inches wider, and whatever weight he carried, it wasn't fat.

Motherfucker looks like he's head of the Aryan Nations at Coxsackie, Khalil thought. Where does Temple get these people?

As Khalil approached, Jeremiah walked up, embraced him, and pounded his back with affection.

"Welcome back, my brother. We miss you in the Bronx."

"I miss you too, brother. Who's your friend? That's the biggest white man I've seen outside the joint."

"That ain't no white man. That's Julio. He's Puerto Rican. He's another one of Temple's students. He's getting a PhD from NYU and on the side, runs the hottest nightclub in East Harlem. I wouldn't fuck with him, though. He grew up in the Smith Projects on the Lower East Side, where if you got blond hair and blue eyes, you got to be extra bad. Trust me. He is."

"I believe you. Muthafucka is huge."

Jeremiah walked Khalil over to Julio and made the introduction. The two men looked each other in the eye and pounded fists, the Lower East Side and the South Bronx sizing each other up. Only in the heat of action would they learn to trust one another.

"Let's go meet Temple," Jeremiah said, walking Khalil and Julio to a black Lincoln town car he had rented for the occasion.

They drove up the Van Wyck to the Grand Central and took the

Triborough Bridge to the Bronx, where they wound their way up the Grand Concourse to 150th Street, stopping in front of the G Bar. Jeremiah gave the keys to the valet and they entered the bar, where Temple was sitting at a round table in the far left corner with two arresting women—one black, one Latina. The black woman was dark skinned, with short hair, long colorful earrings and a tight jet-black blouse over her ample chest. She had a serious expression on her face. The Latina woman was slim and brown skinned, with an Afro and a white low-cut top. Tears were running down her cheeks. Despite being strikingly attractive, both these women had a "Don't fuck with me or you die" look on their faces. Something was clearly very wrong in their world.

"Khalil and Julio, meet Rosa and Monique. Rosa is my secretary and personal assistant, and the best hip-hop promoter in the Bronx. Monique is one of the city's most talented poets, and if she gets her act together, is going to be a great high school English teacher. But we aren't here to organize a poetry slam. We have business to take care of. Rosa, why don't you explain what is going on."

"It's my daughter, Cee Cee," Rosa said. "Girls in my project are harassing her and beating her up on the school bus, in the hallways of her school and on the street. She doesn't want to leave the apartment without me. And when I talk to the mothers of the kids, they laugh in my face. I need someone to put a stop to this and Professor Temple says you know just how to do this."

"We're dealing with a special situation here," Temple added. "The mothers of these girls are all part of the Crips gang that runs the drug business in the Edenwald Houses. They resent Rosa because she is a leader of the tenants' association in the projects, which is trying to stop the Crips from intimidating the working families, who are still the majority in Edenwald.

They figure if they keep harassing Rosa's daughter, Rosa will move out and they can control the whole project. We are going to give them something to think about."

"How we going to do that?" Khalil asked.

"Jarvis Washington runs the Edenwald Crips. Tomorrow afternoon, the People's Justice Cadre is going to pay him a visit. We are going to teach him a lesson about how to run his business responsibly. When we're done with him, Cee Cee, and other children of the working families, will be free to ride the school bus, and walk the projects without fear."

Everyone at the table nodded as Temple continued. "We are going to divide into two teams: one all men, the other, all women. The men will visit Jarvis Washington, the women, the mothers of the girls who have been harassing Rosa's daughter. I have two brothers from Brooklyn, and a sister from Queens coming to join us. We're going pretend that we are undercover narcs conducting a raid. I have badges for everyone and two Crown Victorias to take us up to Edenwald. We meet tomorrow at three p.m. in front of Jeremiah's apartment building. Everyone should wear dark clothing. Are you down?"

Without a moment's hesitation, "Yes," was the unanimous answer.

"Then go back home and prepare. I will take care of the bill."

Rosa and Monique went back to Rosa's apartment, Julio to his bar, and Jeremiah and Khalil back to Jeremiah's apartment. Nelson Temple stayed behind.

On the drive back to Jeremiah's apartment, the two young men were silent. They didn't know the exact plan, but it had to be pretty complicated, and probably pretty violent, because intimidating a Crips leader who ran the drug trade in an entire project was no joke.

After a ten-minute drive, Jeremiah parked his car and Khalil followed him into the building on Faile Street where Khalil had spent a week before he left for Canada. Both men were accustomed to turning to hip hop whenever they needed to relax or build up their courage, and that is exactly what they did now as they prepared for their mission for the PJC. As Khalil plopped down on the living room couch and took note of the books and revolutionary posters that covered the walls, Jeremiah connected his iPod to the small sound system that sat on the living room dresser.

"You like Nas?" Jeremiah asked.

"Hell yes," Khalil replied. "Nobody tells stories better than he does. When I listen to him, I feel a little less crazy."

"Well, here is my Nas mix," Jeremiah said, turning on the sound system and pulling out a joint and a lighter from his pocket.

"Take a hit. We definitely need to calm down before tomorrow."

"Pass it on, my brother. I live on that shit in Canada. It probably keeps me from killing someone in frustration."

The two young men passed the joint back and forth as Nas boasted of his lyrical prowess and the miracle of urban survival in a nation that tried its best to render him and others like him in the like country invisible.

It ain't hard to tell, I excel, then prevail
The mic is contacted, I attract clientele
My mic check is life or death, breathin' a sniper's breath
I exhale the yellow smoke of buddha through righteous steps
Deep like The Shinin', sparkle like a diamond
Sneak a uzi on the island in my army jacket linin'
Hit the Earth like a comet, invasion
Nas is like the Afrocentric Asian, half-man, half-amazin'

Cause in my physical, I can express through song
Delete stress like Motrin, then extend strong
I drank Moet with Medusa, give her shotguns in hell
From the spliff that I lift and inhale, it ain't hard to tell...

"Damn, Jeremiah," Khalil said, sniffing the weed. "That brother is strong. He makes it seem our lives mean something."

"They do mean something, Khalil," Jeremiah replied. "We didn't jump through all these hoops, and dodge all these bullets, just to go quietly into the night. We got to take a stand, both for ourselves, and for all our people."

"Is that what the People Justice Cadre is doing?"

"Word. We give people hope that they can win some battles, rather than losing all the time and killing one another in frustration." Jeremiah took a puff and continued. "Look, Khalil, people in the hood have no real government. There's no one to protect them from corrupt police, politicians who put every halfway house, shelter and garbage dump where they live, legislatures who pass drug laws that ensure their kids go to jail. When our neighborhoods are dangerous, they wall us off and send us to jail. When our neighborhoods become safe, developers come in and kick us out. No matter who is in office, they put our needs last."

Khalil nodded as Jeremiah went on, his voice gathering force. "The PJC is there to even the odds. We give people in the hood an option when their backs are against the wall. Sometimes we use computers, sometimes we use guns, but whatever weapons we employ, we use them only to bring resources to poor people and black people that this racist system keeps them from having."

"Word," Khalil chimed in. "You know, a year ago, I would have said you were crazy, but after spending time with Brother Jamal talking about the movements of the sixties, what you say makes a lot of sense. The best way to help our people is to bring together the street soldiers and the thinkers. The Panthers tried to do that in the '60s, but they made the mistake of telling the man what they were doing, which was like giving an invitation to the pigs to wipe them out. The PJC way is much better. Keep everything secret, do what has to be done, and then disappear!"

"Damn, Khalil, Temple was right. You are one smart brother. Now, let's finish up these J's and get some sleep. We have a busy day tomorrow."

Khalil fell asleep on the couch, and awoke ten hours later, feeling calm and refreshed. He didn't fear what lay ahead. For the first time in his life he felt everything that he had been through had happened for a reason. The power he had acquired through stress, pain, and hard testing could be used to relieve pain in others.

When noon came, Khalil and Jamal began getting ready. Slowly, they put on the dark clothes that were their uniform for the day, and made sure their weapons were ready: for Khalil, his .38, for Jeremiah, his knife.

Twenty minutes later, the two men heard the squeak of tires and muffled voices from outside in the street and saw two dark blue Crown Victorias double-parked in front. They headed downstairs and piled into the second Crown Victoria, where Julio sat with two tall, light-skinned black men, Ryan and Richard, two former Lehman basketball players from Queens that Temple had befriended. Julio gave all four of the men police badges and told them to put them in their pockets.

In the meantime, Temple entered the car in front where Dee, Monique, and Molly, Temple's former prize research assistant who had come up from Queens, sat. Molly was a short, strong-looking, young white women.

When Temple gave the signal, the two cars headed up Faile Street to Southern Boulevard, and drove to the intersection at Boston Road just South of the Bronx Zoo. Then they drove up Boston Road for about two miles into the Northeast Bronx, passing rows of fast food restaurants, body shops, appliance stores, and stores carrying Caribbean products.

On the side streets stood rows of two- and three-family brick homes, with an occasional four-story apartment building. By Khalil's standards, this looked nothing like a ghetto, but there were as few white people on the streets as he saw in the South Bronx. At Gun Hill Road, the caravan made a right turn and after several blocks made a left on Baychester, passing several blocks of two-family homes and a Catholic high school, before they got to a huge complex of red brick buildings ranging from six to fifteen stories in height. This was Edenwald Houses, the housing project where Rosa lived. Khalil was stunned.

"This is a housing project?" he asked. "This neighborhood looks like it could be in Canada. People in Patterson would eat these motherfuckers up."

"Don't underestimate these folks," Jeremiah warned. "They're feeling the recession just as much as people in Patterson and have to deal with the same shit jobs, corrupt politicians and brutal cops that poor black people everywhere have to face in this motherfucking country."

"Gentlemen, enough sociology. We've got work to do," Julio interrupted. "Put your badges on, have your guns ready, and prepare to run full speed for the first building on your left. We are going to sprint through the main entrance, run up the stairs to the fourth floor, and break down the door to 4P. Jarvis Washington should be there holding a meeting with one of his lieutenants. Khalil and Jeremiah, you are going to take Washington captive while Richard, Ryan and I are going to deal with his associate. Keep your eyes open. You may witness some things you've never seen before and may never see again."

Everyone in the car nodded. Before Khalil could take a deep breath he heard Julio's deep voice again.

"Okay," Julio said, "one, two, three, now—GO!"

The five men leapt out of the car and ran full speed toward the project building with guns out, a battering ram in Julio's hand. As Khalil sprinted, he saw the people in the project walkways run for cover like they had seen this all before. They were sure doing a great imitation of neighborhood cops.

Khalil followed Julio though the door to the stairwell and sprinted up the four flights of stairs. Julio turned to his right and ran full speed with the battering ram toward an apartment at the end of the hall and smashed the door down with one powerful motion. The five men burst into the apartment to find two black men sitting at a bridge table with thousands of dollars in large bills in front of them, along with several plastic bags of white powder.

Before they could get at their guns, Jeremiah had tackled the well-dressed man on the right, while Ryan and Richard had secured the large, rougher-looking man on the left. Khalil moved quickly to put a gun to the head of the man who Jeremiah tacked, and they quickly disarmed him and moved him to the plush white leather couch that sat in the adjoining room.

"Now the fun begins," Julio said.

"Do you know who we are, Mr. Washington?" Jeremiah asked.

Khalil kept his gun to the man's forehead. Given the circumstances, he looked surprisingly calm.

"Fuck no. I've already paid off the neighborhood cops, so I figure you must be Feds. But the Feds don't care what happens in Edenwald. Is some motherfucker running for President?

"We're not cops. We're not Feds," Jeremiah said. "Think of us as the Black Panthers come back to life, only stronger. We're street niggas on a mission. And our mission today is to get the Edenwald Crips to stop threatening Rosa and her daughter and let the Tenants' Association do their work. We don't care if you sell drugs, so long as you leave Rosa and people like her alone."

"Damn nigga!" Washington yelled. Even with a gun to his head his dark face filled with calculating rage. "Who you think you are, trying to tell me how to run my business. If I do what you say, every young nigga in the projects is going to try to take me out. Here in the hood, respect only comes through fear."

"Well, Mr. Washington, we agree on one thing," Jeremiah said, shoving Washington forcefully back into the couch. "Only it's you who is about to learn a lesson. Watch what we do very carefully and then see if you still want to avoid a deal."

Motioning toward the other captive, Jeremiah turned to Julio, Richard and Ryan.

"Take that nigga's clothes off," he instructed.

While Washington's lieutenant screamed in rage, Julio put him in a headlock. Richard and Ryan removed his clothes. Within less than a minute, the man was completely naked. He was almost completely unconscious as Julio kept squeezing harder to prevent any resistance.

"Now, take out the sign and tie it to his dick," Jeremiah called out.

At that point, Richard pulled out a twelve-by-twelve cardboard sign, with a long piece of string attached that read, 'People's Justice Cadre', on both sides in large black lettering. While Julio kept squeezing until the man could barely breathe, Richard tied the sign to the man's long, flaccid penis.

"Now, walk him to the living room window," Jeremiah commanded, looking in Washington's eyes, which suddenly had a look of both fear and amazement. "And open the window all the way."

"So, Mr. Washington, before our final act of the day, let me tell you who you are dealing with. We are the People's Justice Cadre. Think of us as the gang to end all gangs, except we are not interested in money, we are only interested in one thing, justice. We are tired of our people being beaten down, and we have decided to fight back. We take on the rich and the powerful and we also confront people who live in our neighborhoods and who be doing the Man's work. Right now, you are doing the Man's work and that has to stop."

Washington sat speechless, his eyes darting back between his naked lieutenant, his soldiers on the ground, and Jeremiah.

Not receiving a response, Jeremiah nodded to Khalil who dug his gun in closer on Washington's forehead.

"So, Mr. Washington, are you going to deal with us or not?" Jeremiah continued.

On that signal, Julio, Richard and Ryan moved the terrified man to the window and pushed him out, only stopped from falling by the powerful grip Julio retained on his ankles. As the man screamed and cursed and cried for help, Jeremiah and Khalil walked Washington to the window and told him to look down. Below him, under the window, were a group of ten women, held at gunpoint by Monique and Molly, while Dee, Temple and another woman looked on. They all looked like they had just been invited to their own funerals.

"Now, Mr. Washington," said Jeremiah, you have seen what we can do. Are you going to tell the people who work for you to leave Rosa and her daughter alone?"

"Yes, Jesus. You people are fucking crazy. I don't want anything to do with you. Just get the man up out that window and put some clothes on him. And you can have the drugs and the money. Just get the fuck out of here."

"We don't want the drugs and the money. We just want you to do your business differently," Jeremiah said.

At that point, Julio pulled the man up through the window and threw him on the floor.

"Get dressed, muthaucka," Julio said, while Richard kept a gun trained on the man's head.

"Here's the deal. The head of the People's Justice Cadre is coming up to see you with one of the organization's lawyers. They are going to give you a piece of paper to sign, which says that neither you, or anyone who works with you, will have anything to do with Rosa and members of her family. In return, we are going to provide you with some skilled legal assistance that you might need in your business."

"I don't want your help," Washington said, bitterly.

"Brother, you ain't the enemy because you sell drugs. You the enemy because your drug dealing gets in the way of our community being organized and able to fight for its rights. You do your business in a responsible way, and we will help you. You don't, and we will kill you. Get it?"

"Got it," Washington said.

At that moment, the door opened and Temple walked in with Rosa and a tall curly-haired woman in her early fifties.

"Hello, Mr. Washington," Temple said. "My name is Nelson Temple and I am a professor at Lehman. This is my associate Jean Monahan, the best criminal lawyers in New York. I assume you know Rosa, my secretary?"

Washington nodded.

"You are going to sign a statement taking personal responsibility for the safety of Rosa and every member of her family. I realize that is an act of extreme generosity on your part, but that generosity will not go unrewarded. From now on, whenever you or any of your associates are arrested, you can call Jean or one of her partners to represent you in court. You can be sure that you will do much, much better than you are doing now with your current representation."

"And why should I believe any of this, Mr. Temple?" Washington said.

"Because Temple will kill you just as soon as he would order a cup of coffee," Khalil blurted out. "It could be your dick out that window, only your body won't be attached to it. Trust me, you want to sign off on this deal as quickly as you can."

Washington nodded to Joan Monahan who brought the legal papers for Washington's signature. After signing, he nodded to Rosa, who walked over to Washington and shook hands with the Crips leader.

The deal was sealed. As long as Washington was running the drug trade in Edenwald Gardens, Rosa and her family were safe.

Khalil took in what he had seen and smiled. Whatever might happen in the future, he was no longer a victim. Live or die, it was going to be on his terms. He and Rasheeda had taken a huge risk, and freed themselves. Now he had the privilege of freeing others. Canada might be nice but it wasn't where he belonged, and soon Rasheeda would have to realize that. Khalil touched the scar on his face. It was a mark of his trials—experiences he would never again try to forget.

He was **PURE BRONX.**

MELISSA CASTILLO-GARSOW | MARK NAISON

AUTHORS

Mark Naison is Professor of History and African American Studies at Fordham University. He is the author of four books and over 200 articles on African American politics, labor history, popular culture and education policy. Dr. Naison is the Principal Investigator of the Bronx African American History Project, one of the largest community based oral history projects in the nation and has begun work on an book of oral histories from the BAAHP, with Robert Gumbs, entitled *Before the Fires: An Oral History of African American Life in the Bronx from the 1030's to the 1960's.* His articles about Bronx music and Bronx culture have been published in German, Spanish, Catalan, and Portuguese as well as English. He has two books coming out this year, a novel *Pure Bronx*, written with Melissa Castillo Garsow, and a book of writings on education and youth activism, *Badass Teachers Unite*, to be published by Haymarket Press.

When not doing historical research, Naison likes to play tennis and golf, post commentary on his blog, "With a Brooklyn Accent," and make periodic forays into the media. During the last five years, he has begun presenting historical "raps" in

Bronx schools under the nickname of "Notorious Phd" and has been the subject of stories about his use of hip hop in teaching in the *The Daily News*, Bronx 12 Cablevision, and Fox Business. He also comments regularly on education issues through his blog and on LA Progressive, History News Network and *The Washington Post* "Answer Sheet, and is one of the founders of three education activist sites on Facebook -"Dump Duncan," "Occupy Teach for America" and the wildly successful "Badass Teachers Association." However, some know him best for his appearance on the Chappelle Show, where his "performance" has been preserved on that show's Second Year DVD.

Melissa Castillo-Garsow is a Mexican-American writer, journalist, and scholar currently pursuing a PhD in American Studies and African American Studies at Yale University. Her short stories and poetry have been published in various journals including *The Acentos Review, La Bloga, Hispanic Culture Review, Hinchas de Poesia* and *The 2River View.*

Melissa completed her Master's degree in English with a concentration in Creative Writing at Fordham University in 2011 where she was a graduate assistant for the American Studies Program. Prior to that she was awarded a Bachelor of Arts from New York University summa cum laude with a double major in Journalism and Latin American Studies. A former employee of NBC News, El Diario/ La Prensa and Launch Radio Networks, Melissa has had articles and reviews published in a wide variety of forums including *CNN.com, Latin Beat Magazine, Washington Square News, University Wire, El Diario/La Prensa, Women's Studies, Words. Beats. Life: The Global Journal of Hip-Hop Culture,* and *The Bilingual Review.*

Melissa is an active scholar in the fields of English literature, American Studies, African American Studies and Latin American/Latino Studies. At Yale, she focuses on the study of Afro-Latino history and culture in the 20th Century, presenting at numerous conferences across the country. This is her first novel. To learn more visit www.melissacastillogarsow.com

PAPERBACK BOOKS

MAIL US A LIST OF THE TITLES YOU WOULD LIKE INCLUDE **$14.95 PER TITLE** + SHIPPING CHARGES $3.95 FOR ONE BOOK & $1.00 FOR EACH ADDITIONAL BOOK. MAKE ALL CHECKS PAYABLE TO: AUGUSTUS PUBLISHING 33 INDIAN RD. NY, NY 10034

▲
DEAD AND STINKIN'
STEPHEN HEWETT

▲
A GOOD DAY TO DIE
JAMES HENDRICKS

▲
WHEN LOVE TURNS TO HATE
SHARRON DOYLE

▲
IF IT AIN'T ONE THING
IT'S ANOTHER
SHARRON DOYLE

▲
WOMAN'S CRY
VANESSA MARTIR

▲
BLACKOUT
JERRY LaMOTHE
ANTHONY WHYTE

▲
HUSTLE HARD
BLAINE MARTIN

▲
A BOOGIE DOWN STORY
KEISHA SEIGNIOUS

▲
CRAVE ALL LOSE ALL
ERICK S GRAY

▲
LOVE AND A GANGSTA
ERICK S GRAY

▲
AMERICA'S SOUL
ERICK S GRAY

▲
SPOT RUSHERS
BRANDON McCALLA

▲
THIN LINE:
A CHILD'S EYE NEVER LIES
ANTHONY WHYTE

▲
NAKED CONFESSIONS
TRACEE A. HANNA

▲
PURE BRONX
MARK NAISON PhD
MELISSA CASTILLO-GARSOW

▲
IT CAN HAPPEN
IN A MINUTE
S.M. JOHNSON

HARD WHITE
SHANNON HOLMES
ANTHONY WHYTE

STREET CHIC
ANTHONY WHYTE

BOOTY CALL *69
ERICK S GRAY

POWER OF THE P
JAMES HENDRICKS

STREETS OF NEW YORK VOL. 1
ERICK S GRAY, ANTHONY WHYTE
MARK ANTHONY, SHANNON HOLMES

STREETS OF NEW YORK VOL. 2
ERICK S GRAY, ANTHONY WHYTE
MARK ANTHONY, K'WAN

STREETS OF NEW YORK VOL. 3
ERICK S GRAY, ANTHONY WHYTE
MARK ANTHONY, TREASURE BLUE

SMUT CENTRAL
BRANDON McCALLA

GHETTO GIRLS
ANTHONY WHYTE

GHETTO GIRLS TOO
ANTHONY WHYTE

GHETTO GIRLS 3:
SOO HOOD
ANTHONY WHYTE

GHETTO GIRLS IV:
YOUNG LUV
ANTHONY WHYTE

GHETO GIRLS 5:
TOUGHER THAN DICE
ANTHONY WHYTE

GHETO GIRLS 6:
BACK IN THE DAYS
ANTHONY WHYTE

LIPSTICK DIARIES
CRYSTAL LACEY WINSLOW
VARIOUS FEMALE AUTHORS

LIPSTICK DIARIES 2
WAHIDA CLARK
VARIOUS FEMALE AUTHORS